The Last Sorcerer

CHRISTOPHER HEARD

Harracott Publications

First published in Great Britain in 2007
Harracott Publications
Harracot Farm
Frithelstock Stone
Torrington
Devon EX38 8LA

ISBN 978-0-9554802-0-1

Cover illustration by Philip Dixon, Mill Street, Torrington, Devon.
Cover design by Thurbans Publishing Services, Hindhead, Surrey.
Printed in Great Britain by Cromwell Press, Trowbridge, Wiltshire.

For Mum and Dad

Characters

Shyam   (pronounced *shahy-am*) Shyam is an associate of the Black Mages and is a practised demimage. He has a strong rivalry with Eldred, so strong that he is willing to stop Eldred from losing his powers. Shyam currently waits patiently, under his master's will, for the right moment to strike.

Eldred   (pronounced *el-drid*) Eldred is a sorcerer, one of the last few after the Great Revolt. He was reckless in his younger years, but as time has passed he has become wiser and more powerful. It is Eldred's task to find the last student, one who is prophesized in his master's prophecy. He had once saved Shyam's life and currently holds a rivalry with him.

Mr Alden   (pronounced *ohld-en*) Mr Alden is an elderly man, who lives on the outskirts of a town, besides the Twilight Canyon. It was here that he witnessed a duel between a sorcerer and a demimage, Eldred and Shyam.

Master Alim   (pronounced *ah-lim*) Master Alim is a demimage, one who has lived well past his expected age. He is the owner of the Academy of Alim, where he teaches demimages and also a singular sorcerer, named Eldred. Master Alim gives Eldred a prophecy of both a new and last sorcerer, who will help save the kingdom.

Melanie   (pronounced *mel-uh-nee*) Melanie is Leonard's aunt. She wants the best for her nephew, but finds it difficult to relate to him. When a strange incident occurs in their home, she asks Gregory to do what he can.

Leonard	(pronounced *lee-oh-nahrd*) Leonard is the main character of the tale and is a farmer with no memory of his parents. He lives with his aunt and uncle, where he spends everyday helping them. Little does he know, he has a much greater destiny than any man could predict. He will soon realise his awaiting destiny as his sorcerer powers begin to emerge...
Gregory	(pronounced *greg-uh-ree*) Gregory is Leonard's uncle and is a hardworking farmer. After a strange incident in the household, Gregory is led to believe Leonard is a demimage.
Sarah	(pronounced *sair-uh*) Sarah is a young lady, a year older than Leonard, who was abandoned and birth and fostered to adulthood by Eldred. She has spent her years at the Academy to both become an excellent archer, a skilled herbalist and has some demimage ability in healing.
Alexander	(pronounced *al-ig-zan-der*) Alexander is a Flamedra, an ancient race that has lived underground and has the ability to manipulate fire. Alex was sent to the surface by his clan to discover the secrets of their race, and it is Alex's dream to learn how to create fire so that he may teach his brethren. Although young in appearance, Alex's age is completely unknown.

Terms

Demimage *(pronounced dem-ee-meyj)*. A person trained in the magical arts. Unlike a sorcerer, they use an item infused with dragon blood to use magic, typically a wand. The name demimage was derived from sorcerers, and means 'lesser mage'. This was to show their ranking in power, as the sorcerers considered to be much more powerful. A demimage, unlike a sorcerer, is able to use their emotion to cast spells. The Great Revolt was started by the demimages.

Sorcerer *(pronounced sawr-ser-er)*. A person trained in the magical arts. A sorcerer is a person with a draconic heritage, and as such has dragon blood in their veins. This blood allows the person to cast spells naturally using only their mind and magic. A sorcerer requires a disciplined mind to cast his spells and must have control of his emotions to prevent his spells going awry. A sorcerer who uses his emotions will become tainted and their soul darker, even perhaps evil.

Flamedra (prounounced *flam-edra*). A rare, underground race of humans who were blessed by a god, giving them the power to control fire.

Contents

Publisher's Note

It must be noted that the author conceived this when aged 14. For this reason, the publishers believed that it should not be 'heavily' edited by a professional editor, an adult, who would interpret and change the presentation to meet the style and standards required of a book written by a mainstream adult author. The novel does not suffer as a result and is a remarkable achievement.

This is a great novel and maybe the first of a series. *The Last Sorcerer* should appeal to all aficionados of this genre.

I

Duels and Destiny

He couldn't take it any more. The light shone strongly through the murky window, the sounds of people fighting outside added to his stress, leaving him no chance of sleep. Grabbing his long coat, he dashed outside. He was already grumpy from the bright light; all he wanted was some peace and quiet. He had to stop the noise! Whoever they were, they were going to see what happened to them when he got really annoyed. Mr Alden rushed over to the edge of the rock–filled chasm below his home, breathed deeply and then looked below. Definitely not a pretty sight.

"Right you!" Alden cried, "If you. . . " BANG!

He stopped. Was that – was that fire? He could have sworn that a great ball of flame had come from the bushes deep below and smashed into the rocks on the far side. He shook his head. Nonsense: that's impossible. It must have been a trick of the light. But wait. . . the light! He looked down further and there was a man, glowing as though he was an angel from heaven. The man had long, shining brown hair tied in a ponytail. He carried a long sharp spear in one hand and his other pointed to the far side of the chasm, about fifty paces away, waiting for something. . .

"You can't hide in the darkness. . . " the figure of light shouted menacingly. "Show yourself, Shyam; you cannot hide from the light." With those words, a dark figure launched itself from the bushes and landed in the middle of the rocky chasm. The figure had long black hair, blowing in the wind, and a striking look in its red eyes. The man of light below smiled.

"You know that is not my name, Eldred!" Shyam hissed as he brushed his hair back. But his words sounded false. Eldred remained smiling, almost arrogantly, while twirling his spear in his fingers. Shyam laughed darkly.

"You think you are powerful?" Shyam snarled. "But no, too much good in you. . . too overconfident. . . too reckless. . . I'll show you what happens when you meddle with the likes of us."

"Not tonight," Eldred countered. "This night will bring de-

9

struction upon you. You do not deserve to live and I shall make sure of that!"

Shyam gave a serpent's hiss, raised his hand, and sent a vivid sheet of light towards Eldred from his fingertips. The glowing orb of intense energy surrounding Eldred deflected it into the sparkling night sky.

– 0 –

Alden thought that he had stepped into a dream. Was this true? He just stood there, transfixed, as if petrified by the strange and mystical energies that were blasted from two apparently ordinary people. Shards of ice and bolts of lightning almost blinded him. He hoped that he had fallen into a nightmare. But there was no mistaking the destruction of rocks and trees as each continued their assault. The sounds and smoke obliterated everything else. No matter what either of these combatants did, each evaded the other with agility and blocked the attacker.

It must be a spell, Alden thought: a trick of the mind. Wait a minute... a spell... these are spells! And powerful by the looks of them! He knew that there were powerful elders who had magical abilities in this land, but these two seemed far too young. What *was* this devilry?

– 0 –

Shyam leapt at Eldred, yelling with obscene aggression. But now they fought with conventional weapons – spears. They cursed each other loudly. Shyam's spear swept across Eldred's cheek, immediately splattering dark red blood across the rocks. But Eldred was ready: he got close enough to touch Shyam's face and a great flash of red light engulfed them. Shyam yelled in pain, falling to the ground where he lay screaming in agony. He writhed around clutching his face. When Eldred moved his hand away from Shyam's face, Alden saw a horrific sight. A blistered and distorted face that had turned a bloodless white with all life sucked away.

"If only you could see yourself, Shyam. Your face – you will have to live with it for all your life," Eldred said, wiping blood from his cheek.

"This isn't over yet!" shrieked Shyam, standing up slowly and painfully. He touched his own face and the blisters vanished, yet the lifelessness of his face remained.

"It is, but only for you," Eldred replied, his spear rising level with Shyam's neck. Shyam laughed loudly.

"Oh *dear*! My face, *my poor face* is ruined!" Shyam mocked him loudly, "It does not matter what has happened now. I know who you're looking for, and I *will* stop you. I need you to remain my rival."

"I am always your rival. And there is little point trying to stop me, I do not even know where she is." Eldred replied, keeping his spear raised.

"You may be my rival now, but if you found her you will fall like I did. Don't throw away your talent so easily," Shyam said. "In telling you this, is my life debt repaid?" He grimaced at the very thought of the debt he once had, but now his swollen eyes wondered along Eldred's spear.

"Yes," Eldred replied, looking into his rival's face. Eldred tensed his arm and thrust the spear towards Shyam's neck in a killing strike. But too late! In an instant, a hazy black smoke surrounded Shyam just as Eldred attacked and... Shyam was gone! No body, no trace, nothing! Eldred cursed loudly and threw his spear in anger at the ground where Shyam had stood. He sat down upon a rock and took a large slurp from his water –skin – the golden light fading from his body. He sighed heavily and then attended to his bleeding cheek.

"That'll leave a scar," he muttered angrily to himself standing back up. Then, his emerald green eyes caught sight of a small wooden stick lying abandoned on the ground. It was shaped like a wand, made of polished oak with a colourful inlay of a fiery design curling around it. Eldred picked it up and smiled.

"Ah... a demimage should never drop his wand." He quickly put it in his pouch and then stretched his arms out wide. Instantly, his body reappeared in front of Mr Alden on the chasm's edge.

"Now..." Eldred turned and looked directly at the stranger. Mr Alden, still in shock, gulped and ran to his house door. But Eldred beat him there with another of his spells.

"Aaaaaaaah!" Alden cried and tried to run away. His body froze. What the – he had been frozen in mid-air and couldn't move at all! His eyes seemed to be the only thing moving – just like in dreams. Eldred turned to him, now almost nose to nose.

"I demand you release me," Mr Alden said.

"Hello, nice to meet a friendly face." Eldred clicked his fingers, and now Alden's whole head could move freely.

"What are you doing?" Alden cried loudly. Eldred placed a finger to his lips, silencing him.

"I'm just pondering over what a person like you is doing watching a person like me?"

Alden's lip was trembling, for Eldred's voice was so bold. Eldred continued to smile happily, tilting his head as if Alden was something in a cage.

"Who – who are you?" Alden managed to fearfully stutter through trembling lips, his forehead now dripping with beads of sweat.

"There will be little point in you knowing, but as you seem so distressed: my name is Eldred. I am a demimage of these lands and a thwarter of evil. I do not wish to harm you." He said this very quickly, but Alden held on to every word. Then Alden replied quite bravely:

"You're not a demimage, are you?" he said quietly, staring straight into Eldred's eyes. Eldred continued to smirk but moved slightly away. As he did this, Alden's body returned to normal and he was now standing back on the ground.

"Your initiative serves you well. No, I am not a demimage. I am in fact a – " He stopped.

"A what?" asked Mr Alden quizzically, one of his eyebrows arched. Eldred's smile faded and he turned his back on Alden.

"Never mind, old man," Eldred mumbled, starring blankly at the mossy cliff top. Alden then suddenly leapt back.

"FIEND! You are a sorcerer!"

Eldred turned in a blink of an eye, grabbed the scruff of Alden's collar and lifted him off the ground, pinning him against the house wall. Their eyes met sharply.

"You know too much," he growled. He placed a finger on Alden's forehead and then Alden collapsed to the ground in a deep sleep. Memory wiped and in a slumber. The sorcerer's easy way to escape such an unfortunate event. It was a shame that sorcerers still had to hide these days. Things were a lot better before all of this. Eldred opened the oak door, picked Mr

Alden up, and placed him on the small wooden seat in front of a large, brick fire. There was a rustle. Eldred hurried outside, closing the door silently, and then took his spear and observed the area. Another rustle: he had stayed too long.

"That darn Alden, always doing something to wake us..." mumbled someone, coming up from the hillside. Eldred picked up a dried leaf on the ground and placed it in his palm. The leaf seemed to melt into his hand and he felt his legs lift from the ground and he was gone from the awful place. Winds were swiping his whole body as he zoomed through blurs. The blur began to calm. His feet had landed in a small chamber room and, he knew, he was back home: the Academy of Alim.

$$- 0 -$$

The room was quiet and the smell of gardenias engulfed Eldred's small button nose. He was in the large entrance hall that had a shiny white marble floor and mahogany walls. He took off his scorched robes (for Shyam had burnt them); waved his finger and the burns magically vanished, along with the outer robe itself. He made his way through various corridors and past dormitories of sleeping demimages, for Eldred knew his teleportation spells would not function within the Academy. Eventually, he came upon a solid gold statue of a dragon. He placed his hands upon each of the wings and spoke in a strange tongue. The statue slid to the right, revealing a large marble archway before him. A large spiral staircase led him up ever higher to the tallest tower of the academy. Eldred sighed and rested upon the bannister of the staircase, twiddling his spear in his fingertips and watching an old man who was sitting on a crimson and gold trimmed mat, meditating silently.

"Ah... hello there, Eldred, a most eventful night you have had, have you not?" the man said coarsely, opening one of his dark brown eyes. Eldred bowed deeply and quickly sat down cross-legged opposite the elder.

"Yes, Master Alim, I was attacked by a – " Eldred was stopped as Master Alim placed a finger upon Eldred's lips.

"First, help me up, I must rest my body," Master Alim murmured, grasping his oak staff and leaning against it. Eldred leapt up off the ground and helped his ageing master. He

13

supported him across to the plush, red cushioned sofa and carefully helped his master to sit.

"Now, explain." And so, Eldred told him of being stalked by Shyam through the woodlands, and then the duel that began. In extreme detail, he told his master what Shyam had said and decided it best to keep the peasant Alden, from Master Alim's ears. Master Alim sat still for a few moments, meditating again as he analysed the information he received. He gasped.

Eldred felt it too. There seemed to be nothing around them, but a strange, invisible draft of magic could be felt by both of them. Eldred simply stood, wide-eyed at the strange feeling that now echoed around them. There was a feeling of mystery, but also great magic that filled the air around them. Unexpectedly, the feeling suddenly spread away from Eldred and instead was vacuumed violently into his master. Master Alim fell to the floor, clutching his chest and gasping for even the smallest breath. Eldred watched in disbelief when his master then cried out aloud in pain – then became silent. Eldred stood frozen, unable to think of what to do or say.

"The seal!" Master Alim cried loudly, with what little breath he had, his eyes spinning in divining power. "The door will be opened!"

"One to open – open the door... no wonder – NO WONDER!" he shouted at the height of his voice in a violent fit, his breathing continuing to get heavier. Eldred stood there, petrified and horrified by the sight of his old and weakening Master.

"Light soul... soul light... the way to hell's gates... infernal calls! No one will survive: NO–ONE!" and with the final cry he collapsed on the sofa, his breathing steadied and his spasm calmed. Eldred fell to his knees, his eyes watering. That was no ordinary fit. Eldred gazed at his master with watery eyes. He was afraid, fearing for his master. Master Alim could have died. And for the first time, Eldred knew – with trembling hands – that it would not be long until his poor tired Master would walk the golden stairs...

– 0 –

A faint chipping sound could be heard. Eldred stirred slightly, and then he slowly opened his drowsy eyes. He was still in his master's tower. Looking up, there was Master Alim, standing proudly alongside an obese, moustached man who was chiselling away at a huge boulder. Maybe it was all a dream, thought Eldred. He raised himself up from the ground and walked over to Master Alim, rubbing his eyes.

"Ah... good morning, Eldred. Did you have a nice nap?, he asked kindly, not removing his eyes from the chiselled rock. "Not that my floor is the best of places to be sleeping..."

"Yes, Master. What is this?" he asked curiously, pointing at the rock. Master Alim now drew his eyes away from the rock and his eyes now met with Eldred's.

"This rock is to engrave the prophecy I made last night," he said simply, "that way when I am gone it will not be forgotten."

"So it wasn't a dream last night. But, Master, it looked more like you were having a − a spasm, rather than a prophecy?"

"Hmm, I did not realise that my body was moving so much. The prophecy that I made, dear Eldred, was not one for the purest heart. It holds secrets to a new evil and a concealed curse. That is why my body reacted so violently to it: for you see, the body is linked to the mind and both are affected." Eldred nodded, only understanding slightly what his Master had said, and then looked back at the rock. The first few words had been engraved in by the expert chiseller.

"When will the engraving be ready?" said Eldred.

"Hopefully by noon: and the faster the better, Enriqué."

The man, Enriqué, gave a small grunt and then continued to chisel away at the rock. Master Alim gave a small chuckle, followed by some wheezing.

"Eldred, would you please come with me?" Eldred nodded and then followed Master Alim through the passageway out of his master's tower.

There were many cherry blossom trees in the academy gardens, all in full bloom. It was because of these trees, that Master Alim most enjoyed spring. He would dearly miss the spring...

"Eldred, do I look old to you?" he asked softly, as they walked slowly through the gardens. Eldred hesitated, and then spoke.

"Of course not," he replied unconvincingly. It was a lie. Age is such a burden. Master Alim had grown very old, wrinkling and becoming ever weaker. Not even his most mystical magic could put a stop to death.

"Yes I do... of course I do," he replied simply, sitting himself down on the fresh grass in the refreshing shade of the trees. Eldred sat down beside Master Alim and looked to the sky. Dark rain clouds were beginning to cover the sky.

"Tell me, Eldred. What did Shyam mean when he asked whether his life debt was fulfilled?" Master Alim asked.

"When he was still here, as a student, I saved his life," answered Eldred. "I am not surprised he would want to rid a debt from me, now that we have become enemies." Both Eldred and Master Alim sat quietly for a few minutes, left to their thoughts.

"Nevertheless, he will now wish for vengeance and your crimson blood. You have made yourself a difficult and deadly rival. A servant of the Black Mages is not a good choice for someone as young as you."

Eldred sighed sadly. His master still didn't think he was strong enough. Then he felt something sharp prodding him in the leg. He quickly pulled out a short, decorated wand from his robe pouch: Shyam's wand.

"Master, I present to you with the wand of Shyam," Eldred said, in a kneeling bow, "I did not realise I still had it." Master Alim smiled and raised Eldred's chin so that he could see.

"Keep it. It will be a useful artefact in the future. For a demimage's wand is like a samurai's katana. The samurai's sword is his soul and the same for a demimage and their wand." Eldred looked at the wand curiously as his master spoke.

"But, couldn't Shyam have another one made?" Eldred asked, placing the wand on the ground.

"He could, but his soul would be broken into pieces. Their soul is bonded to their wand. If he did make more tools, his soul would keep breaking. To lose a fragment of his soul, Shyam will lose power. That is why, a demimage is weak." Master Alim explained bluntly. Eldred starred at him, in great surprise at what his master had said.

"But – but *you* are a demimage, and – and you are not weak!" he exclaimed loudly, surprised that his master had just insulted himself. Master Alim smiled.

"You wield a greater power than a demimage. You need no support to wield your powers, for you – "

"That's not true! I needed your help! If it wasn't for you I would be dead!" he shouted angrily, even though his master had complemented his power. His master sighed.

"Nevertheless, Eldred, you *have* grown powerful: more powerful than any demimage at this academy," Master Alim complimented. "And even though I, a demimage, have raised you to control your skills, you still despise demimages themselves. Why?" Eldred didn't speak. He instead starred into the sky, peering at the pearl clouds.

"I – I don't want to talk about it."

"What is it you fear, Eldred? Why is it that you will only trust me and no other? Why is it that you retreat from the world? Why, Eldred! Why?" Master Alim shouted firmly. Eldred didn't reply.

"I see," Master Alim finally said, giving up, "Perhaps one day, I will know why. But not in this lifetime." Eldred suddenly turned to him drastically. Did he just say what he thought he said? But that would mean...

"Master..." Eldred said feebly.

"I have grown sick, Eldred. And like all things in this world, we must pass. Not even the deities can stop that," Master Alim said calmly, his eyes watering slightly. A bright, ravish pink flower fell in front of them both.

"The petals of a cherry blossom are like life. When the blossom blooms, that becomes the peak and greatest time of your life. Then, the petal falls, just as everybody's life must crumble away." Master Alim turned and looked at Eldred, whose eyes were blotchy and watering. Master Alim placed a comforting hand on Eldred's cheek.

"Fear not. For that will only lead to suffering. I do not fear the afterlife. Heaven, hell, rebirth: it does not matter. But Eldred, I ask one thing of you."

"Anything, Master... I shall do as you command," Eldred said, lips trembling and eyes draining great tears.

"My time has come and the great torch must be passed on," Master Alim explained with a coarse voice. "To you – I give you this academy to use it as you will. But more importantly, more important than anything else, is the prophecy." Eldred gave a watery laugh.

"I knew you were going to say that."

"Yes, Eldred, I suppose you did," Master Alim said quietly,

with a gentle laugh, "But please, this prophecy holds the secrets of the future. A great evil could rise and then there will be one person to unite the kingdom. Find this individual and train him." Eldred nodded sadly. Master Alim's head began to waver slightly, but he kept talking through iron will, "And most importantly, there is – is something important. A tool... the Soul Light. Find it – in my mind I heard... a voice... telling me of its importance. Use it to help the – the new one.

"He will – he will be the – the last – of – of your – your kind...' And the final breath had passed from Master Alim's body. He collapsed in Eldred's lap, and Eldred cried long that day: the day in which he would no longer see his master. He had gone to a better place, away from the awful things to happen in many years time. He would no longer have to suffer, nor fear, nor hate. Eldred was alone. The person, who had once been like a father to him, was gone. He was gone... forever...

– 0 –

Eldred buried, through pain and sorrow, the empty vessel of his master. Many of the academy demimages came to grieve, but none really knew him like he had done. He highly doubted that even the High Mages of Asgarth who visited his burial knew him, not in the slightest. He knew it was best to keep the prophecy with his master. And so, he levitated the stone tablet down upon Master Alim's grave site. The black clouds began to thunder and great splashes of rain heaved down on Eldred. Now Eldred was the master. His destiny had been revealed to him and he knew what he must do.

"I will not fail you, Master. Tonight, it begins...' And Eldred stood in the rain, realising there was no time for fear or doubt. The great stone tablet before him: this was his key. The key to finding the last glimmer of hope for the great realm of Asgarth:

He will open the door
Leading to light and soul
Destruction and war
The fiery hole
And the gates of doom
He must conquer all fear

18

Or be sent to his tomb
With all he keeps dear
Last of the line
Too great and too few
It will be his shine
That will solve the clue
To empty the wagon
And end the fight
Son of dragon
Heir of light

II

Unknown Gifts

Dazzling sunlight, radiating heat and dry, dusty ground; not good for a farmer's crop. There hadn't been rainfall for a week now. Leo, however, couldn't really care less. It was about time something *different* happened around Yarnsdale; even if it was just a drought. Boring, boring, boring... that's what it was. With a world of bold knights, mystic mages and fearsome fiends why was it that he ended up in this tiresome and tiny village? Every day, Leo's uncle forced him to work on the crops, keeping the crows away and then feed the poultry and animals.

Leo, who was sometimes called Leonard, was of a strong build. Perhaps with all the farm work he did, he had simply become naturally tough. His eyes were green like emeralds and his brown hair was down to his neck, wave–like and interesting. Yet, the thing Leo most liked about his hair were the two blond streaks at the front – they were completely natural, but they made him feel special because he had something different compared to everyone else.

"Stupid uncle," he groaned, wiping his forehead. "What were the chances of ending up with him as an uncle, of all people?" Leo threw around grain for the chicken, who were clucking anxiously in their pen. It still made Leo upset, even now, fifteen years since he was born. He had lost both his parents after he was born. He didn't even know what his father looked like. His mother, however was a different matter. He had a memory of a beautiful, blonde haired maiden smiling down on him...

Leo shook his head quickly. *Better not daydream in case Uncle sees*, thought Leonard, and he poured the rest of the grain out of the sack in a large heap. Now, in his life, he had the misfortune of having a grumpy uncle and an obsessive cleaner of an aunt. Joy to the world...

"If I'd had it my way, I'd have been out of here if it weren't for one little thing," he mumbled to himself, now collecting fresh eggs into a wooden bucket. Well, maybe not little.

"Leonard! Dinner's ready!" his Aunt called from the farmhouse window.

"Coming!" he shouted and hurried back indoors into their tiny kitchen. His Uncle, grey haired and bulky, was sat down at a large oak table waiting impatiently for some food. Leonard sat down opposite him in his own wicker chair and stared at the fireplace. He watched as it crackled and burnt through the wood. His skinny Aunt, meanwhile, was boiling potatoes.

"Leonard," said Uncle, peering out the window.

"Hmm? Yes, Uncle?" replied a dull Leo. His Uncle's eyes returned to the meal in front of him, placed down by his wife.

"What have I told you about piling up the grain? You know you shouldn't." Leo groaned loudly and his Aunt gave him a piercing stare.

"What?" he said innocently. "We all get tired and forget things." His Aunt then peered out of the window too.

"Well if you just listened to your Uncle you wouldn't – " she started.

"Why do I have to do everything he says!" he yelled angrily, slamming down his knife and denting the table.

"Hey! There is no need to talk to her like that!" his Uncle shouted back just as loud. This happened all the time: another pointless argument over the family table. They hadn't had a peaceful meal for months, not that Leo helped that – he tended to stir everyone up.

"Well, everyone treats me like dirt!" Leo cried, pulsating with anger. Why couldn't they give him a break for one damned second?

"That's not true!" his Aunt said, now rising to her usual crescendo.

"Yes! Listen to your Aunt! You don't seem to listen to me anymore!" his Uncle shouted forcefully, stuffing a potato in his mouth.

"Oh... GO LOSE SOME WEIGHT!" Leo roared. He threw down his knife and stormed out of the house, slamming the door. A huge gust of wind seemed to blow through the entire house, blowing out the flames of the fireplace. The furniture and all was sent flying around the room. Both Leo's Aunt and Uncle ducked for cover as knives slammed into the wall. What was going on? This was no ordinary wind, that's for sure! The wind finally calmed and they looked at the destruction of the room. How did – how could Leo of done this? There was no way...

– 0 –

The nerve of them! Why couldn't they give him a break for once in a while? All they seemed to do was nag and nag and nag. Leo growled angrily and continued down the dusty pathway to the bottom corn field. This was Leo's sort of sanctuary field for him, where he could just be with himself. While there he would often peek over the hedge at the manor garden, just in case she was there.

The sun continued to blaze down its fiery heat on Leo. He was glad to finally reach the field. He dived into the corn and took shade under the scarecrow. There was nothing in the sky to suggest strange or terrible things could be happening in a short time. Leo was kidding himself. Something is always going bad in his life.

"If only I were a cloud," he grieved. "I could just forget my worries and hover around." He sighed and sat up to peer over the hedge. The Yarnsdale Manor garden was opposite Leo. A glorious, brick and slate manor house with a garden full of many flowers. Then, Leo's eyes latched onto a young lady, hanging out some wet clothes. Her hair was long and flame coloured, with pink bows in her hair. She was the same age as Leo, according to what his Aunt had told him. Leo sighed sadly. If only he could have some time and talk to her.

You have time now. Leo shook his head. He was too nervous. He lay back down in the corn and pondered for a while. He felt his stomach doing back flips as he thought of what he could do or say. *This could be the only time to talk to her.* He'd have to summon up the courage. Leo hated it when his mind pointed things out. His stomach did another back flip. He had to talk to her...

"Is there someone there?" a delicate voice spoke. Leo's body shuddered in complete shock, causing the top of the corn to waver around him, and she then saw where he was. He heard her giggle, and Leo quickly sprang up. She was wearing an orange taffeta gown and was peering down on him. Leo felt the heat rush to his head and he knew he was blushing.

22

Come on, Leo; say something or she'll think you're simple, or something...

"Hi," he said nervously with a weak smile.

"What were you doing down there?" she asked curiously with a smile. Leo quickly jumped up to his feet and brushed the corn off his clothes.

"Err... I was – I was just – just relaxing," stuttered Leo. Whenever he got nervous he would stutter like a maniac. Just knowing this made him more embarrassed. He tried to calm himself down.

"Oh right," she said, now hanging up the remaining clothes. "My name's Erika. You're Leonard, right?"

"I prefer to be called Leo, thanks," Leo said through clenched teeth.

"Okay then, *Leo*." Erika finished clipping the last dress on the washing line and then leaned on the hedge.

"You don't come down here often do you?" she asked, moving slowly towards him.

"No, not really," Leonard replied blankly.

"Well, I've watched you down here when you've been working in the fields," Erika said. She suddenly realised what she had just divulged to Leo, and quickly looked down at her now twiddling feet, blushing a violent crimson. *She had been watching me?* Leo's confidence grew.

"So... have you always lived here?" Leo asked, desperately making conversation to quell the nervous silence.

"No, we haven't. Both my father and mother came from the north. I was born there and when I was three years old we emigrated into Southern Asgarth," she answered, still starring at her feet nervously. "What about you?"

"Me? Well... I'm not too sure of where I'm from, but I know that I was only a few months old when I came here. Ever since, it's been my Aunt and Uncle and this wretched farm of theirs," Leo exclaimed angrily. Erika looked into his emerald eyes, but her face looked saddened – even guilty.

"It must be hard without your parents," she said sympathetically. Leo nodded grudgingly, lowering his head. He never liked to talk about his parents – he had never known them.

"Hey, keep your chin up," Erika said encouragingly. Leo smiled vaguely.

23

"Besides," Erika continued. "Things can't be that bad."

"Leonard!" a shout bellowed. Leo turned quickly to see his Uncle standing cross armed and glaring at both him and Erika. Leo knew he was in for it this time. He slowly stumbled his way to his Uncle who guided him back to the house. Erika gave a gentle wave as he left and then returned to the manor.

The house door was slammed shut and Leo stared at what seemed to be a nearly demolished kitchen he had once been eating in. There were china pieces on the floor; one of the wicker chairs had broken legs whilst others were turned upside down. A knife was even embedded in the wall!

"Err... been doing some decorating, I see," said Leo, cautiously stepping around the kitchen.

"There's nothing to kid about here, Leo. How did you do this?" Leo's Uncle said sternly.

"Wha – what! How could I do something like this? That is so unfair!" Leo complained loudly.

"Calm down, dear. Gregory didn't mean that, *did you?*" his aunt said, glaring at her husband. Gregory seemed to quickly catch on to her point.

"Oh, of course not!" Gregory said. "It's just – we think that *you* had something to do with all of this, well, catastrophe."

"And why would that be?" Leo said angrily. Gregory sat down on the one remaining wicker chair that was still standing. There was a long silence and his Uncle's face became a face of seriousness rather than his usual anger.

"Firstly, I must tell you something about your father," he said. Leo sprang to life.

"You know something about my father? Why haven't you told me before?" Leo said very quickly, gazing desperately at his uncle. Gregory was a bit taken aback, but quickly moved on.

"Calm down, Leonard, calm down. Now... your father, during his younger years, had become a skilled demimage in his time."

"He was a demimage?!" Leo said excitedly. This was the first time he had ever known *anything* about his father. He just wished his uncle would hurry up – he wanted to know everything.

"Yes, yes, he was a demimage, already. Be quiet! It's getting difficult to get a word in," Gregory complained to his wife. "Now, I know this may come as a shock but I think that, just possibly, he may well have transferred some of his magical ability to *you*." Leo stood there in disbelief.

"Me? No – no I don't want to be a – but... me?" Leo said, completely distraught.

"It seems to be the only explanation for what happened here, Leonard," his Aunt cut in.

"But – but I don't want to be a freak! I just want to be normal!" Leo shouted and then ran upstairs to his room. His Aunt finished dusting up the last of the broken china and threw it out of the window.

"Well," Gregory groaned. "At least he knows now."

"So, what was it you were talking about before?" Melanie asked, brushing her hands.

"Oh yes, I said that I would go to Tameria to see what we could do in case Leonard's strange spurt really *is* magic. The demimages there should know," Gregory explained boldly (and rather arrogantly), as if he were some sort of saviour for Leo.

"But, you heard what he said. Leo doesn't want to be a demimage. So why force it on him?"

"Listen, Melanie, it's for his own good. I know it sounds stupid but what if he had another spurt? And even worse than before! You saw what that strange wind did to this kitchen! I won't have it, Melanie! We can't take any risks!" Gregory argued in retaliation. Melanie sighed and nodded.

$$- 0 -$$

Cock–a–doodle–doo! Leo yawned and rolled over to lie on his back.

"You're such a sell–out, you stupid cockerel." He had hoped that the cockerel would not crow today, not since his near obliteration of the kitchen, anyway. He didn't want to have these strange powers. Now that he thought about it, why did he always wish to become a knight in armour when he was younger? It was every child's dream to become a hero and now he had the chance and didn't want it. Besides, he would never leave whilst Erika was here. Maybe if he was lucky, today, he'd go and see her again.

He leapt off the bed and hurried downstairs to get on with his work. Downstairs, most of the rubble had been thrown out of the window and now there were only two chairs to sit on. His Aunt was sat cutting bread and was humming a gentle tune.

"Where's Uncle?" Leo asked curiously. He was usually eating breakfast when he came down.

"Your uncle had to leave on important business, Leonard," Melanie replied, not meeting his eyes.

"Probably about me, isn't it?" he said gruffly, grabbing a slice of bread and warming it over the kitchen fire.

"Oh no, no," she lied. "He has to fetch an important delivery for the village lord. You know, the father of the girl you had been talking to."

Great, so Uncle had told her about him talking to Erika. That's all I need. Leo ate his bread quickly and then took a quick gulp of ale. Instinctively, he grabbed a bucket of grain and made his way to the door.

"Oh, Leonard, your uncle has done your chores; you don't have to worry about them," Melanie said quickly. Leo was slightly taken aback. His uncle had done all of his work? Most unusual. It was as he placed down the mucky bucket that a sudden spark crossed his mind. A sudden feeling of freedom had engulfed him. He could go wherever he wanted! Perhaps take a look around the village, relax in the fields or maybe – just maybe, see Erika again. This was going to be an interesting day indeed...

– 0 –

A droopy-looking and very tired Gregory appeared at the farm later on that day, carrying a heavy bag holding some strange cylinders with pointed ends; very odd. He heaved the bag onto the table, sending dust everywhere. Melanie appeared from outside just as he sat down.

"Hello dear. How was the journey?" she asked nicely, pouring a jug of ale for her husband from a cask.

"Nightmare," he said briefly, wiping his forehead of sweat. "Blasted mercenaries, always trying to sell ya' something in that god-forsaken place. I tell you, next year, I'm most definitely not going up there again."

"Yes, yes, just have a nice drink, Gregory. You're very stressed out," she said, trying to calm him down. Leo appeared from the front door, gnawing a large chunk out of an apple.

"Hi Uncle, thanks for doing my chores this morning," he said, sitting down beside him. Leo had never been in a better mood. It almost made him want to hug his uncle. Well, *almost*.

"That's okay, Leonard, I thought you'd have the day off for once," Gregory said with a large smile. Leo nodded and then his eyes caught sight of the strange sack.

"Whoa! What are those things?" he said in excitement.

"Oh, these things are called, err – what were they now... oh yes! The demimages called them fireworks or some sort of blabber."

"They just look like a pipe to me," Leo said, picking one up and then tossing it back in the bag.

"Ah, the lord will know how to work them. That reminds me! I best be getting these to him," said Gregory happily. He heaved the bag on his shoulder and hurried out. That was lucky, seeing as Leo usually had to take deliveries himself.

Gregory appeared half an hour later, waterlogged from a heavy shower that had passed, but nonetheless clutching a large bag of coinage. He threw the payment down on the table and wiped his hair with a dirty towel. Not only that, but he took a deep snort at the smell of his wife's cooking.

"I hate rain," he moaned angrily, sitting down whilst Melanie poured him a jug of ale. Leo appeared downstairs quickly enough, smelling the rich smell of boiled potatoes. They all sat down together and began eating their meal quietly. For once – there wasn't a single argument. Shows what happened when Leo got his way...

"Oh, Leonard," Gregory mumbled through a mouthful of potato and steak. "I was given a note for you; don't know what it's about though." He passed Leo a very damp scroll from his pouch. Leo grasped it quickly and put it in his own pouch.

"What would the lord want with me, anyway?" Leo asked. Both his Aunt and Uncle shrugged and continued eating. Leo had thought as much. This wasn't from the lord at all; a much better person. He couldn't help but grin joyfully and quickly dismissed himself from his meal shortly afterward to hurry to his room.

Leo rushed up and clambered onto his bed, quickly taking the drowned scroll from his pouch. On the small piece of parchment was a message scribbled in large, flowery handwriting:

Hello Leo

Can we spend tonight's bonfire party together?
Meet me at the grand oak at midnight.

Erika

Leo simply smiled – this was his chance now, especially if *Erika* had asked him to meet her. Tonight was going to be perfect.

– 0 –

The night sky had turned pitch black, with the peaceful stars twinkling down upon the people. Bonfire night was to be a grand night. The festive fun and dance along with great fires burning high. But tonight, the new invention was to be introduced and who could tell what these strange things could bring?

Leo was fortunate enough to be left on his own when the night arrived. Both his uncle and aunt hurried down to the village to celebrate with the others. Leo made his way swiftly to the highest field on the edge of the village where an ancient oak tree stood. Erika was stood by the tree, looking patiently into the sky.

"Hi Erika," Leo said calmly, jumping over the fence and walking towards her. Erika quickly looked at him.

"Hello Leo, you okay?" she asked kindly. Leo nodded and leant beside her on the tree. She went back to looking up at the sky. "It's such a beautiful night. Don't you think?"

"Yeah, it's – it's nice," he said, stuttering nervously. "So err... why did you want me to come here?" He felt himself blush slightly for asking so directly and looked away from her.

"I just get bored. I'm always locked up by my mother and father," she said sadly and turned to look at Leo. "You're luckier than you think, Leo."

"I – I am?" Leo said, thinking the comment strange or even abnormal. She nodded.

28

"You aren't of nobility like my stuck-up father. He's such a moron!" she shouted angrily. "I don't ever get to leave the house! I have hardly any friends and all I ever do is work like a slave! I mean – why can't they leave me alone?" Leo was slightly overcome by all this. She was spurting out everything and he didn't know how to handle all of this emotion.

"Well, maybe he – maybe he's just – "

"What? Getting me ready for the so-called future that I have?" she shouted loudly at Leo. "He's living his life through me just because his was never perfect! Then there's my mother! Do this and do that! Why can't they just both go away?" Leo looked at her sadly as he watched her eyes water and her lips tremble. Then, before he could do or say anything, she burst into tears. Great drops of tears pouring from her eyes. Leo didn't have a clue what to do. What could he say?

"Are – are – you okay, Erika?" he said nervously. She embraced him suddenly and cried onto his chest. Leo was trembling himself. He quickly placed his arms around her and felt her soft hair, trying to calm her.

After a few moments, Erika wiped the tears from her face. They looked at each other in embarrassment and quickly pulled away, both of their faces blushing red.

"I'm sorry," she said quietly. "It's been stressful." Leo simply nodded, still slightly overcome from being embraced by Erika.

"Look!" she said more cheerfully. "They're lighting the fire!" She pointed down in the distance and sure enough a lit torch was being placed on the wood. The gentle glow slowly became a roaring inferno and bathed the entire village in orange light. Both Erika and Leo sat down together watching the flames, but Leo's eyes seemed to be attached to Erika. He finally turned away to watch the bonfire's flames flicker and sparks fly. Then, a great rocket whistled into the air and exploded loudly into a shower of golden and ruby sparks.

"Wow!" Erika gasped. "It's so beautiful!" Another two spun upwards and a silver shower filled the night sky.

"It is beautiful," Leo said quietly. "Just like you." Leo's gut must have fallen out of place. Did he – did he just say that? Erika slowly turned to face him. They each looked lustfully into each other's eyes. She began to lean in and Leo instinctively did so too. They were slowly getting closer. He kept his eyes fixed on her perfect, blue eyes. He could hardly see her nose – yet could almost count every freckle. Her delicate lips were almost touching his...

"ERIKA!" Both Erika and Leo span around at the roaring voice. The lord was there, glaring furiously at Erika and even more so at Leo. Erika quickly got up and ran to her father. Erika took one last look at Leo and then both she and her father were gone. This was all Leo's fault. He felt the guilt rise as he thought of the punishment she'd receive. He'd have to do *something*. He got up and hurried down to the village. All he had to do was say it was his fault – just anything to stop her from being hurt.

He finally reached the village, but everyone was crowded around the fire so much he could hardly see. He shoved his way through the people and reached the front. He looked up with distress at Erika, as her father dragged her in front of everyone.

"Well then, everyone! Look at this! My daughter, my very *own* daughter... there she was in a field with a filthy little peasant boy!" The lord shouted. The crowd laughed and whistled him on. Leo stood there petrified. She seemed to be in so much pain. The lord gave her a swift kick and threw her to the ground.

"There she was! About to even *kiss* this pathetic farm boy! You don't deserve to be in my honourable family line you wretched – "

"Leave her alone!" Leo shouted bravely, running forward. But the lord, instead of stopping, simply smiled menacingly at Leo.

"Well, now – speak of the devil! Here's the little twerp! I should have you cut from limb to limb!" The lord shouted angrily, and he pulled out a long sharp rapier from the sheath on his belt. "But first, I'll let you watch me punish this little girlfriend of yours, hmm?" He took a slash at her across the back. Leo starred at the blade angrily, looking at the blood on the sword. He felt the rage pulsate in him. The lord raised his arm to slash again.

"NO!" Leo roared.

The lord's body lurched suddenly and the lord yelped as his body began flailing in the air. His rapier flew from his grasp and everyone's eyes became transfixed on the lord and Leo. Leo let out a roar of anger and flew the lord magically straight into the bonfire! He screeched in pain as the flames ignited his regal clothing. A few of the men pulled the lord quickly out and the lord started rolling around to extinguish the flames. But the flames wouldn't die. They grew ever stronger. His posh clothes burnt away and great scorch marks covered his body. Leo's eyes glowed red with vengeance and he continued to stare. One word escaped his lips, like a hiss. *"Die..."*

All of the people watched in fear as their lord burnt and Leo stood vengefully, his eyes like a serpent devil.

"Leo...' a faint voice spoke. "Leo, please stop." It was Erika. Leo's mind clicked and he was back. The glow of his eyes faded and the lord finally extinguished the flames. Everyone looked at Leo. The only sound was the crackle of the fire as he looked around in shock at everyone. His uncle and aunt looked distraught and didn't dare look at him. The townsfolk who had gathered were looking at him in shock and scornful horror. Yet, his heart stopped as he looked at Erika. She looked at him, in the most hideous, befouling way. That look – a look that seemed to be of pure hatred and animosity. That tender moment upon the hill – it was nothing more than a memory now for him. Leo could feel his eyes fill with sorrowful tears. All he had wanted was that tender moment and instead – instead it had led to the breaking of his heart. He looked around, almost whimpering like a puppy, for one last hope in the crowd. There was no–one; there was nothing for him here anymore.

He took one long agonizing look at Erika; turned – and ran.

III

Eldred's New Student

The night sky continued to darken the long stretches of woodland. The stars twinkled and the moon shone down onto mature willow trees, the leaves glittering in its beams. Neither the trees or stars had predicted any great or terrible things for the tear-struck Leo.

Leo continued to sprint through the woods, his eyes blinded with tears and his head lowered ashamedly. He could still hear the angry cries from the village folk. But, worse than that, was the stinging image of Erika's face. He didn't care whether he ran into the trees or even a wild bear. He didn't care if the bear killed him; he just had to get as far away from Erika as possible. His heart had split in two and he just wished he could fall over and die. The pain was horrific. He tripped and smacked his head onto the muddy ground. But he got up, despite cutting his leg, and continued running. The stench of drying mud and blood aggravated his nostrils and his eyesight blurred unevenly.

Another five minutes passed and the voices finally died away. Leo could hardly believe the villagers would chase him. It was just too barbaric! The image of their raised pitchforks and their cries to slay him kept him running desperately. And they had called him both a demon and fiend.

Leo fell flat onto the ground, exhausted, and rested his bruised body against a willow tree. He cursed as the pain of his leg finally got to him. Thick droplets of blood dripped onto the ground and a small, rouge puddle of blood slowly formed.

"Erika... why?" Leo mumbled, his eyes fading. "Why? Why that face..." Leo could still see a vivid image of her angered face and smacked the ground harshly.

"WHY?" Leo cried angrily. His head tipped forward and long crystal tears fell from his swollen cheek. "I don't – don't understand – what is happening to me?" Leo continued to cry sadly and felt his body go numb. His whole body slumped to the ground and he groaned from the pain.

"What is – is happening to me?" he repeated, in confusion.

"When will it end?" The ground around him faded. The darkness had taken him...

– 0 –

A soft chirp came from the corner of the trees. Leo opened his eyes slowly and painfully. If only he could have slept forever – he wouldn't have to worry about anything... but no! This stupid and pathetic world had to wake him up! Why couldn't he be left alone for once? He pulled his body up against the same tree as the night before and heaved his left leg up. He cursed and looked at the wound. It had clotted over – but it was still so painful.

"Stupid tree," Leo said angrily. "They're always tripping me up." His leg seemed to bend at a strange angle. He had broken it. Realising this, he grabbed some nearby branches and started making a cast for his leg, using the flexible vines along the ground to wrap around his leg. He slowly limped away from his spot, mumbled angrily every time his leg hurt, and stopped occasionally to rest. He couldn't stand being a weakling. He was supposed to be tougher than this. Yet, even now, Leo knew that his emotions were the weakest of any persons. That image – an image of Erika. He still couldn't lose it. He pondered momentarily if he could just die from depression.

If only, Leo thought. He continued to limp further and further from Yarnsdale. Why had his life been such a bad one? Isn't there a reason for everything? Or is it just a figment of his imagination and that there are no powerful deities? Leo shook his head fiercely.

No, there must be more to life. He could see the sunlight growing like strands of roots in front of him. He was nearing the wood's edge – he was ever so close.

Just a bit further – you're nearly there.

There was a faint growl. Leo turned, terror-struck, and looked straight into the bright yellow eyes of a large, wild wolf. It growled hungrily and snarled at Leo, with dribble hanging down in long lengths. Leo let out a cry and tried to run. The wolf lunged at him ferociously, clawing his shoulder and tumbling him over. Pain exploded in Leo's leg, for the wolf had broken his cast! But there was no time to worry, as the wolf leapt at him again.

This is it, Leo thought. *I'm going to die; no more suffering.* He dropped his arms, presenting his weakened body to the wolf. The wolf snarled as it leapt into the air and moved in to tear his feeble neck...

A strange and mystifying light suddenly surrounded Leo, covering his entire body like a warm blanket, flinging away the wolf. The wolf crumpled in a pile in front of him, squealing in pain. It jumped up to its feet and fled, whimpering back into the woods and not daring to look back. The light faded from Leo's body and he collapsed onto the ground, clutching first his bloody shoulder then his broken leg.

Why? He thought. *Why do I keep saving myself...?*

Leo became aware of a man in the distance, wearing bright emerald robes and clutching a long stick of some sort. Leo looked up at the figure and then fainted, his head dropping to his ground. The man hurried to the young adult before him. He raised a strange, clicking device over Leo. It started clicking rapidly and the entire tool seemed to fizzle and crackle into the air, vanishing away. The man grinned happily.

"I've found you," said Eldred.

– 0 –

Something glinted above him – something golden – like a butterfly. He tried to grab it, but his arms couldn't move. Then, Leo realised the wings weren't flapping at all... huh?

He blinked. Light filled his eyes as blurred images around him gradually cleared. The first image was that of a young woman, who looked no older than himself. She looked down at Leo and smiled.

"Morning, sleepy-head," she said cheerfully, brushing back her long, vivid black hair. Leo pulled himself up and looked around. He was in some sort of healing room. The air smelt clean and fragrant with the smell of flowers. Huge glass walls surrounded him and through them, he could see long plains of grass and in the distance a forest. Many beds with blue silk covers filled the room. Then he was alone, except for one other person.

"Who – who are you?" Leo asked nervously.

34

"Oh – I'm Sarah. And you're Leo, right?" she said, bobbing her head to the side and looking at him. Leo nodded. How did she know his name? Leo removed the sheet on top of his body. His leg – wasn't it broken? He brushed his hand along the fine hairs over his leg. He stretched it out a couple of times. It had been broken – he knew it had been...

"What's wrong?" Sarah asked, looking puzzled.

"My leg was broken, wasn't it?" Leo asked. Sarah shrugged, pulling up Leo's shirt sleeve and looking at his shoulder.

"Don't think so... was that why you had those sticks on your leg?"

"Yeah, it was. I swear my leg was broken though!" Leo shouted, completely convinced. Sarah laughed slightly at his comment, and pulled down his shirt sleeve.

"Well, don't worry anymore 'cause it ain't," she smiled, standing up and looking down at him with amber-brown, pretty eyes. She sat down on the bed beside Leo's and brushed her hair back again.

There was a nervous pause as they sat beside each other. Leo didn't have a clue where he was and he was with this girl who he hardly knew. She seemed nice enough though...

"So, what exactly are you doing here anyway?" Sarah suddenly asked very directly. Leo sighed sadly and turned over onto his side.

"It's not important," he mumbled. He looked back up to see Sarah looking at him sadly. "Look, don't get sad about it. It's just – just – oh, never mind."

"It can't be that bad – besides, we all have our reasons for being here?" Sarah said, starring up at the tall ceiling. "Or are you just another stubborn boy, huh?" Sarah stamped a foot down angrily.

"Sorry," Leo mumbled nervously. He didn't mean to hurt her feelings. Sarah looked at him for a moment then looked back at the ceiling, twiddling her feet.

"Listen, don't worry about it," she said calmly. She stood up and stretched her back. "Best be off then – you need your rest."

"Wait a minute!" Leo cried desperately. "There's something I need to know – where exactly am I?" Sarah sighed and sat down again.

"You're in the Academy of Alim. It was once an academy for

demimages to learn and practise magic," she explained.

"What do you mean, it *was?*" Leo questioned Sarah.

"Well, it's been nearly 20 years since it shut according to Eldred...'

"And who's Eldred?" Leo asked stubbornly.

"Eldred," began Sarah, "is a sorcerer. He's been the owner of these halls ever since Alim died. I'm sure you'll meet Eldred at some point."

"Okay, thank you," Leo finished, lying back down. Sarah stood up again and moved towards him.

"I like your hair," she said, twirling a finger in his long brown hair, particularly down the blond streaks of his fringe.

"Err... thanks?" said Leo, slightly taken aback. Sarah giggled and then walked out, waving to him. *That was weird,* thought Leo. He lay himself down comfortably onto the bed, and the heaviness of sleep overtook him. *That girl was nice, though. I wonder if I'll see her again...*

– 0 –

The sun was shining down onto Leo while as he lay motionless in bed. He didn't know how long he had been waiting for this sorcerer. It seemed to take forever for anything to happen, just waiting in his bed. No one had come in – not even Sarah.

Leo sighed in aggravation. Maybe he should just leave... no, that wouldn't solve anything. He pulled his body up from under the covers and got onto his legs. His body wobbled as he walked, his arms swinging wildly as he tried to keep balance. His body was very weak from not walking for so long. He lost his footing and fell over, crashing onto the floor.

The doors of the room sprung open and a tall, quite scruffy looking man walked in. The top of his head had tufts of white hair here and there. His face was most peculiar – Leo wasn't sure whether it was wisdom or knowledge that could be felt – but there was definitely a sense of spirit.

"What are you doing on the floor, Leonard?" he asked, pulling Leo back up to his feet. "Sit on the bed for now; you might feel a little bit better."

"Are you Eldred?" Leo asked slowly, seating himself on the bed beside his own. The man, Eldred, nodded.

"Yes, I am Eldred. Tell me, how do you know my name?" Eldred's voice had a peculiar gentleness, and Leo felt more comfortable around him.

"Sarah told me," answered Leo.

"Ah yes, nice girl, isn't she?" said Eldred. Leo nodded. Eldred stood up and paced along the bed.

"She has always been a nice girl," Eldred said softly, "she deserved a much better life..."

"What do you mean?" Leo asked quickly. Eldred looked down at the tiled flooring. There was a moment's pause as Eldred composed himself, then looked up at Leo.

"The poor thing, I believe she was abandoned by her parents at birth. She was simply abandoned in a sprawling city and must have been on the streets for nearly a week. I still wonder how she survived – only just born and on the streets of a busy market place? Who knows what could have happened to her!

"As the week ended I had come upon her on my daily visit to an alchemy stall at the market. I saw her and quickly took her, trying to find her parents. I couldn't find them, so I had no choice but to take her with me. From that point on, she has never left my side and has stayed with me at the academy. She's been here ever since, and she isn't an ordinary human either." Eldred looked at Leo's grazed arm.

"That wound was much deeper," said Eldred, pointing at Leo's arm. "But she helped it heal. She's a demimage and is very skilled at healing magic. Some times things like bruises or cuts simply disappear from the moment she touches the wound with her wand."

"Is that why you became so fond of her?" asked Leo, intrigued.

"Well, that and also that she's like a daughter; never met such a nice young lady in my entire life, either. Gets a bit stressed, being the only girl, but nevertheless a kind person." Eldred sat in silence for some time, deep in thought. Then Leo spoke to break the silence:

"She told me you're some sort of demimage?"

"Oh no, not a demimage – a sorcerer," he replied. Leo looked at him in confusion.

"And, err... there's a difference between a demimage and a sorcerer?" asked Leo rudely. Eldred laughed heartily.

"Of course there's a difference! But don't worry about that now, for I have questions to ask *you*, Leonard," Eldred said happily. He clapped his hands together and leaned in to take a better look at Leo.

"Tell me, do you happen to come from Yarnsdale?" asked Eldred quickly. Leo looked at him in shock, and then fearfully nodded.

"So, you're the one the villagers were shouting about nearly a week ago?"

"Yes, they chased me into the woods, calling me a demon among men. I had to run, there was no–one on my side," Leo explained sadly, painfully reminded of Erika. Eldred nodded as Leo explained and quickly sat down opposite him.

"And, if you don't mind me asking, what did you do that inflicted such a violent attack and made you flee?"

"Well, I sort of – well, I set the lord on fire," said Leo shamefully, not daring to look at Eldred.

"How did you set him on fire? I have a feeling it wasn't by normal means; am I right?" asked Eldred abruptly. Leo nodded

"Okay. So how *did* you catch the lord alight?" Eldred asked, almost excitedly.

"I'm not sure, but I just felt, I guess I felt angry. And when I looked at the lord he just caught on fire. But I remember the feeling – it was like a furious rage. I wanted him dead because ..."

"Yes?" prompted Eldred. Leo stuttered for a moment, and then said: "Never mind, it's not important."

Leo simply sat on the bed, his head hung low and his mind dwelt on Erika. He could still feel the depression and the will to die inside of him. If only he hadn't been such an idiot... he could have done something...

Eldred stood up suddenly. Leo looked up in surprise, and Eldred was smiling excitedly. He was actually smiling! Here's Leo, depressed as a slug, and there's Eldred looking like the happiest man in the kingdom!

"Get dressed Leo; I have something you will want to know. There's some clothing in the trunk under your bed." Eldred walked over by the door looking through the window as Leo changed into a blood-red shirt and some navy tights from the trunk. He buckled two black boots on and then hurried over to Eldred. Eldred led him through a long, musty corridor and then through two huge oak doors, which were heavily decorated with images of trees and exotic creatures. Then, a huge gulp of fresh air filled Leo as he stepped into what he thought was a garden suited for heaven. Huge trees with small, pink petals were all over the garden, with a stone path and many beautiful flowers of all kinds filling the field. Many different smells swept into Leo's nose as he walked with Eldred along the stone path.

They both followed the path silently until Eldred stopped in front of a huge, stone tablet. Leo looked up at the giant tablet, catching a glimpse of the words upon it. Before he could finish, however, Eldred moved on and Leo followed grudgingly.

"You're not normal, Leonard," said Eldred, pacing along the path.

"I figured," Leo said grumpily. "Why does it matter to you, anyway?"

Eldred finally stopped, and sat himself under a large oak tree. He said: "I want to show you a new world Leo; a world without borders or limits."

"What do you mean?" asked Leo, kneeling down beside Eldred on the earth.

"What happened in your town was no mere accident, Leonard. You are obviously very potent in what can only be described as *The Art*," Eldred explained, starring up at the cloudless sky.

"*The Art?*" Leo asked, intrigued. Eldred smiled, nodding his head.

"Yes, Leonard, *The Art* is the art of magic, practised by all sorcerers and demimages!" Eldred looked at Leo's expression. But it wasn't what he had expected. He wasn't excited or entertained; he was sad. "Is there something wrong, Leonard?"

"It's just," Leo said, sighing, "I just don't know if I want to be a demimage. I don't know if I want to get into something like that. I just – just don't know...'

"Listen, Leonard," said Eldred softly, "I won't pressure you into anything. If you don't want to learn magic, I fully understand. Just remember one thing for me."

"What's that?"

"You're not becoming a demimage." Eldred laughed quietly to himself, but this small comment actually cheered Leo up slightly.

"Are you even *going* to tell me the difference between the two?" Leo asked, smiling.

"Mm... maybe... depends on something though. Do you want to learn to be a sorcerer or not?"

Leo stood up suddenly and started walking towards the healing ward. His mind was still hurt from the previous week's events and there was much to consider. Leo said quietly: "I need some time."

"I understand," said Eldred. "I can see your mind and heart have been badly hurt. Take as much time as you need. I stand to my word: I won't pressure you to hasten your decision. Just make sure you make one." He winked and then stood up, huffing in the effort.

"Eldred? If you don't mind me asking, how do you know about how I feel?" Leo said, startled by Eldred's knowledge.

"I have a keen talent for such things, m'lad. Now, if you don't mind, I have some things to deal with." Eldred paced away, but softly, under his breath, he muttered: "Poor thing.'

– 0 –

Leo found himself in the healing ward once again. He didn't know how long he had been there, but it felt like forever. Just lying down on the bed with nothing to do but to think about people and events. He just couldn't make a decision about what he wanted to do. Part of him ached painfully for Erika, whilst the other wanted to kick the memory into the nearest gutter.

Leo sighed angrily and rolled over to face the ceiling. Why can't he just get over her once and for all? But the worst thing was the painful reminder of how he had felt whenever he pictured Erika's face. Even when he felt nervous or excited, he always had that gut feeling. It was such a strange feeling like he would be happy for all eternity. But in one moment, it was crushed...

Leo couldn't take it anymore.

I'll go, he thought. *Clear my mind, and then maybe come back and start*. He pulled out the trunk from under his bed and started putting in the few things he had in it. Leo looked at the tiny amount of things he had. He couldn't work with this. He had no money and hardly any clothes. Heck, he couldn't do anything if he got *attacked*.

Leo sat down beside the open trunk and looked up through the window into the deep skies above. He just didn't know what he wanted anymore. *Stay here... do it...* his mind would urge, but he just couldn't empty his mind of all the painful memories.

"Wait...' Leo whispered, "... they're just... memories." It was like a bubble in him had suddenly burst in relief. He was right. It didn't matter any more. They were just harmless memories!

"Staying then?" a voice sprung up. Leo suddenly looked towards the oak doors. Eldred was standing there, arms crossed and leaning against the door frame. Leo nodded excitedly, receiving a just-as-excited smile in return.

"Come with me," said Eldred, "I will explain everything."

IV

The Blood of the Sorcerer

There was a peaceful silence in the morning as the dawn of day emerged from its slow and tiresome sleep. The chatter of winter robins filled Leo's room, along with a gentle breeze that swept from the window-ledge.

Leo rubbed his eyes, waking himself from his drowsy state. He jumped up from his oak bed and began changing. Eldred had kindly given Leo his own room to stay in with his own private belongings. Leo quickly changed into some of his work clothes and hurried outside into the magnificent garden where Eldred was to meet him.

Just as expected, Eldred was sat patiently against one of his blossom trees, and Leo hurried over to him.

"Good morning, Leo," said Eldred. "Got some sleep?"

"Some, but I was too excited to sleep most of the night," Leo replied. Eldred simply smiled at him.

"You'll be getting your sleep after tonight. Probably won't find magic as exciting as you'd expect, either..." Eldred forced himself up with his rickety staff and then placed a comforting arm around Leo, guiding him as they walked together.

Instead of following the usual gravel path, Leo found himself drifting from the path with Eldred into a large, open yellow corn field. In the distance, Leo could just make out the image of a large person seated in a ring of red candles, each burning gently. As they drew closer, Leo could see his flame-red scruffy hair and strong physique. His face and skin were tanned, with bold cheeks and ginger eyebrows that were long and thin.

"Eldred, who is that?" Leo asked, still staring at the boy. Eldred peered over at the boy.

"Ah yes, haven't met Alex yet, have you?" Eldred said. "He's my other student, beside Sarah, and an interesting student at that."

"Why's that? Is he a demimage, too?" Leo asked.

"Not at all; he's a *Flamedra*."

"Err... a what?" Leo said, confused. Eldred sighed, rubbing his head.

"A Flamedra is a creature of fire, and Alex is a – "

"He isn't human?" Leo exclaimed loudly. Eldred ushered him to be quiet.

"Careful now, best not let him hear that. Alex is very short-tempered. You know what they say about redheads, huh?" Eldred whispered quietly. Leo nodded embarrassingly.

"Anyway," Eldred continued, "a flamedra is a being of fire. It was rumoured the god of fire, known as Vulcan, blessed some humans with arcane powers over fire. They became the race known as the Flamedra. They bred secretly away from human contact and over time have become a race of their own. I only knew about their existence because of Alex.

"Alex asked me to meet with him after hearing about my master's academy. Of course, my master had died, but I continued on training myself in secret. Alex asked me to help him develop his powers, and in return he would tell me about the Flamedra." There was a moment's pause between the two. Then Leo said:

"But, what does he need to develop? He has the power of fire! What more could he want?"

Leo then noticed Eldred looking over at the cross-legged Alex. Amazingly, the tiny flames from each of the hot, melting candles grew in length, rising into the air above Alex. Slowly, they joined up, becoming a huge, burning ball. Leo blinked and the fireball was gone...

"A lot more..." answered Eldred. "He manipulates fire, but can not create it. That is what he seeks: creation. When he finds it, he will disappear back to his homelands. Then, we will see nothing more of him." Eldred gave a small wave to Alex. Alex looked at Eldred, then interestingly at Leo. He simply nodded sharply and continued his practise.

– 0 –

'So, shall we begin?" Eldred asked, smiling. Leo nodded impatiently. This was what he had been looking forward to all night. Eldred smiled and stood opposite Leo. Eldred simply stood for a moment, then clicked his fingers.

Spears protruding from the ground appeared, and the flattened corn below Leo's feet vanished and became solid rock.

43

Many chalk rings surrounded Leo, with him in the centre.

"How did you – how did you *do* that?" Leo gasped in amazement, spinning on the spot looking around himself. Eldred swirled his finger, spinning a purple puff of smoke from nowhere.

"Magic," Eldred winked. Leo stood stiffly in the centre circle as Eldred paced around him.

"This is a training circle," Eldred explained slowly. "In this circle is you, and only you. As you progress, you move into a new circle and new things are taught. Eventually, the final circle becomes the much dreaded world that we are in. From now on, the only importance is this centre circle."

"But what about..."

"*Nothing* lies outside the centre circle!" Eldred suddenly shouted strictly. Leo stood startled, deciding it was best not to say anything.

"Now, let us begin." Eldred paced slowly around Leo, as if inspecting him, and then stood still behind him.

"Firstly, the matter of the demimage and the sorcerer: which is slowly dissipating from the minds of the common peasants.

"A demimage is, like us, a magic-user. However, they rely on tools for their power. I'm sure you've seen them before, yes?"

"No," said Leo, shaking his head.

"They are wands, staffs and rods of mystic powers," explained Eldred. "They could be anything – yet one thing rests in common with such possessions."

"And that would be?"

"They all contain a small essence of dragon blood," said Eldred plainly. He walked around and met face to face with Leo.

"It would be nice if you kept your tongue tied whilst I'm explaining, Leonard. It seems I'm starting to find the real you." He tapped him gently on the cheek, and then hurried towards a spear in the ground. He threw the spear carefully to Leo and drew one of the coarse-wood spears himself.

"As I was saying," Eldred continued. "They need dragon blood because of its magical properties. It is said in ancient lore that dragons were the first known beings to possess magic. Not only that, but dragons could transfigure into humans. This led to dragons actually falling in *love* with other humans. And so, magic passed to the humans.

"This led to sorcerers developing in later generations. A sorcerer is a person who can manipulate his dragon ancestry and tap into its powers, thus," Eldred spun his wrist, and the clouds above him in the sky split slowly, revealing a pool of light around Eldred. "Magic was born."

There was a small gust of wind that swept over both of them, causing their clothes to swing and ripple. Leo looked down at the spear, rubbing a finger along its coarse, dirty surface.

"I understand now," said Leo softly. "But what do I do with this?" He raised the spear up lightly to show Eldred. A tiny smile crossed Eldred's face.

"For discipline."

"For discipline?" said Leo, utterly confused. "What's so important about discipline?"

$$- \, 0 \, -$$

The night, covered in dark cloud, now governed the sky. No sign of a star or moon could be seen as Leo collapsed onto his bed. He was breathing deeply, his lungs and chest burning painfully. He was sorely regretting what he had said now.

There was a firm knock on Leo's door, followed by the door creaking open. Leo looked up not to see Eldred, but Sarah and Alex. They both sat on the side of his bed, where he lay completely worn out.

"Hiya," said Sarah happily. "All tired out?" Leo didn't say anything, but nodded ruggedly.

"Aw... has Eldred been working you too hard?" Alex said, in a girlish and mocking tone.

"Leave the poor guy alone, Alex. You can hardly talk; you were like Leo when you were first here," said Sarah angrily.

"No, its okay," said Leo depressingly. "He's right, anyway. I was worked to my absolute limit." He sighed and wiped his forehead of his salty sweat. "I didn't even practise any magic *at all*."

"Oh... he's doing it again," said Sarah, talking to Alex.

"Hell yeah, what were you expecting?" said Alex loudly. Leo looked at them both.

"Well... you'd think someone could control themselves..."

45

Sarah continued, ignoring Leo. Leo was now getting severely shocked. Had he done something? Did he do something annoying? What on earth were they talking about? Oh great, they weren't talking about *that* were they?

"He has been waiting nearly 30 years for this. No wonder he's got so excited." explained Sarah. Leo almost fainted in relief. So they weren't talking about *that* certain part of his anatomy...

"Who's this you've been talking about?" interrupted Leo quickly.

"Eldred," answered Alex. "He's using an old teaching method on you. Oldest one I know anyway."

"He is?" pondered Leo. "But – well, why?"

"Who knows?" Alex replied gruffly.

"Well, it might be because you're the only known sorcerer in the past fifty years. He probably wants you to be trained properly. He toughens you up before teaching you the magic side," said Sarah, smiling innocently at Alex. She then whispered in Leo's ear discretely.

"I think he's a bit jealous," she giggled quietly. There was an annoyed groan from Alex.

"I heard that...' he said through gritted teeth. Leo simply laughed.

"Don't be jealous! You're a flamedra; that is so much cooler!" exclaimed Leo encouragingly. Leo smiled as he saw Alex's spirit lift a little.

"Maybe...' Alex said, looking darkly at the floor. "But I'm sure Eldred has told you. I manipulate fire I can't create it. That's the worst part."

"You'll make it eventually," said Leo. Alex stood up and walked towards the door.

"Thanks, but no thanks. I don't need any verbal support on this. It's something I have to do alone." Alex walked out, leaving the door slightly ajar and the sound of footsteps gradually faded.

"I best be off then," said Sarah. She smiled at Leo and left, closing the door. Leo smiled happily. Things weren't as bad as he thought...

– 0 –

Many days passed, and what Alex and Sarah had said was

becoming true. Eldred was pushing Leo to the limit. For many weeks it was physical training: sprinting, exercises, stretching. Eldred told him it was important to improve strength, endurance and flexibility. Leo soon found out why.

After the weeks, he was taught *yari–jitsu*, or the 'art of the spear'. According to ancient legend, this art was brought from a distant continent, and the Asgarthian sorcerers made the spear their conventional weapon. Soon, Leo learnt the basics of combat, movements of the body, basic attacks and defences. All these eventually advanced to more complex movements and forms of offence. His former training hadn't finished yet, either.

Over the two months, he had come to know Alex and Sarah a lot better. The flamedra Alex had been at the academy for nearly five years now, but didn't even know his own age. His race had long forgotten about time – for all Alex knew he could be many decades old but in teenage maturity of the flamedra race. Also, over many days, he eventually explained about his heritage from his clan. His clan, located underground, was dying out. He was the son of the head chieftain and he was guided by his father to the outside worlds. Alex's father asked him to learn how to control fire – even if it took him his entire life and the clan no longer existed. Now, Alex pursued this dream and worked towards it.

Leo was wrong about what he had said. Alex was more human then creature. He wasn't after gain; he just wanted his family and clan to survive.

Eldred was right about Sarah from start to finish. She was funny, playful and entertaining. Leo often found himself being cheered up or helped by Sarah when he was down. He had also been healed by her on numerous occasions. One day, Leo asked why she was really here.

"Because Eldred's like a father," she had said. "I want to help him out. Ya' know – it's what friends do."

Surprisingly, even to Leo, he was starting to bond with Eldred. Despite the hard training and the strict etiquette, Eldred was just as normal as anyone else. Often he found Eldred laughing at Leo's mistakes or even at his own. Sarah was right too, he was like a fatherly-figure. He looked after you if you got hurt (and Sarah couldn't heal the wound) or if you had a problem. That didn't mean he didn't get angry, of course!

But for Leo, the thing that was best for him, learning about everyone and having a good time was only second to one thing. He finally felt like he was in a true home and part of a real family.

– 0 –

The pearly-white snows of January had set in. The days grew icy-cold and the training became ever harder. Leo often found himself with frostbite or a streaming cold. But, as Eldred had said many a time: 'No pain, no gain.'

The golden rays of the sun gleamed through the window of Leo's room and woke him from his usual, tired sleep. It was easy to sleep, but annoying to get up. Guess that's what you get for working like a slave every day...

Leo stretched and squinted his eyes at the sunlight coming through his window. He clambered out of bed and then – there was a small parcel.

"What's this?" he mumbled, rubbing his eyes and picking it up. He looked at the label on top: '*From Eldred*'. Leo ripped apart the package and a pile of clothing fell onto his bed. Leo looked at the clothing, amazed: there were large, black boots and black leggings with buckles along the side. Then, there was a cherry red, buttoned shirt. Finally, there was a long, heavily decorated cape of blacks, greens and golds. Leo ran a hand through the silky cape and then examined everything. He could hardly believe it. All of this had been given by Eldred. He hadn't expected Eldred to be so – well, generous. It all looked so expensive too. Perhaps Leo was starting to get better at his training...

He carefully put on his new clothing and then left for breakfast.

Leo made his way through the wooden-floored corridors to the main hall. The main hall was once a place where demimage students would meet and discuss things with each other, or with their mentor. Now, Eldred had simply made it a place for dining. Many long yew tables that were once polished finely where laid up against the walls, each covered in a thick layer of dust. Only one table remained as it had before, where Leo sat himself beside Alex and Sarah.

"Morning," Leo muttered. He fetched himself some bread served on the table and scraped some butter on.

"Hi, Leo," they both answered, Alex mumbling the words through a mouthful of porridge.

"New robes?" Sarah asked, tilting her head slightly to examine it. Leo took a bite from his bread and nodded. Sarah giggled. "From Eldred?" Leo blushed this time and nodded again. Alex examined the clothing too, looking suspiciously at Leo.

"So... he just gave this to you?" said Alex bluntly.

"Yeah, but it was packaged and had a note on it. He didn't really give it to me directly," answered Leo.

"Hmm... but – *why?*"

"I dunno, why does it matter?" Leo said, now grabbing a bowl of hot, steaming porridge.

"Well, this stuff looks pretty expensive," said Sarah, stroking her hand through the silk cloak. "Maybe it's a gift – Alex?"

"Maybe," Alex said gruffly, turning back to his meal. "But Leo's right, it doesn't matter."

Leo nodded, and after about half an hour of talking and eating he hurried outside. A chill ran down Leo's spine as he stepped into the thick snow that covered all the fields. The trees now bare and thin, were covered in thin layers of white. The sun made the snow gleam. Leo could feel his nose going red and the air tasted moist and bitter. Leo plodded through the snow to the largest field where Eldred sat bare-chested meditating... wait a minute, he was bare-chested in the snow! Is he mad? Leo looked at Eldred for a moment, but he wasn't showing any signs of being cold – not even shivering. Eldred slowly opened his eyes and looked at Leo.

"Problem?" Eldred said curiously.

"Err... no, not at all," lied Leo, looking away. Eldred stood up and looked at him.

"You shouldn't lie, you know. That's called a sin," said Eldred. He flung on his own white shirt, clicked his fingers and the snow covered training circle appeared. Leo moved into the centre circle, as always, and awaited Eldred's command. There was silence for a moment, except for the odd robin chirping in the trees.

"It is time to move to the next circle, Leo," Eldred said

happily. "This will be a very interesting circle indeed – and could take either a long or short period of time to complete. We will just have to see..."

"Okay," replied Leo. Leo looked gloomily at the floor below. He counted the rings below him – wait a minute – he was on the last one! He had reached the final ring! A joyful smile crossed Leo's face. Eldred smiled in return.

"Good to see you have come so far. But don't forget the other circles on the inside. If those collapse, then the outer rings will too." Eldred paced around in his usual manner, then stopped in front of Leo.

"Please sit, Leo," he said plainly. Leo sat down cross-legged, looking up at Eldred.

"It is time," he said, "for you to learn the art that is magic. It will not be an easy task to accomplish – but once you do, the only limits are your imagination and that alone."

"So, what do I need to do?" asked Leo.

"A great deal of concentration and also an important factor – belief. If a person believes they can do *anything*, they can do just that: anything. You must do the same, and you will be able to achieve the unachievable." Eldred knelt down opposite of Leo and looked at him with his mystical, green eyes.

"There are some things, however, that I must warn you about," said Eldred seriously. Leo nodded, hanging on to every word.

"Magic requires a clear mind to be done precisely and controllably. A sorcerer was trained, often from an early age, to understand their emotions. For it is our negative emotions that make magic spontaneous and dangerous. Anger, hate, aggression: the emotions of those without compassion and who know nothing of love. When these emotions are released, magic becomes a tainted art. Those who use their emotions in battle eventually become consumed by their hate and anger, tainting their hearts in darkness and fuelling themselves by endless rage. Even positive emotions can be detrimental for a sorcerer, for it prevents the mind from staying clear." He paused for breath.

"A sorcerer does not seek adventure or fortune. A sorcerer works for his master and the people, guiding them, preserving the world around them. In these times, however, the Way of the Sorcerer is slowly being lost...' Eldred glimpsed at Leo for a second, then stood up. Leo remained seated, listening demandingly, taking in every word.

"Stand," he instructed. Leo jumped up and pierced his spear deep into the soil around him. Leo removed the admirable cloak he wore and hung it carefully onto the spear's end. Eldred examined Leo, watching his movements closely.

"Now, I want you to close your eyes," said Eldred, pacing sideways and watching Leo with careful, observant pupils. Leo closed his eyes.

"Feel your senses," said Eldred. "Let the senses of your body fill you and feel the ground, the air, the sounds of the world. . . '

Leo's senses seemed to awaken and a sudden, swift gush of feeling could be felt. The slow drag of his master's footsteps through snow; the gentle and freezing breeze that made his body shudder; the quiet echo of his breathing. He felt his chest expand with air, and then empty. Silence. Leo's body seemed to slant and then. . . he felt something. Leo leaned to the left and snapped both his hands up by his head. He opened his eyes.

He stood, leaning to one side, grabbing the shaft of his master's spear. Leo had just realised what had happened: Eldred had attacked him with his spear! Yet, somehow, his body had known to move out of the way. Eldred smiled, pulling the spear back to his side.

"Amazing," he whispered, taking a step back. "I did not expect you to do it the first time."

"But," said Leo, "that was not magic. How could that be the power of the sorcerer?"

"Strangely enough, it is both as close to magic and as far from it that you can get to it," said Eldred. Leo looked at him, puzzled.

"What I mean," Eldred continued, "is that what you did *is* magic but in a very, very different form. But it is an important step, nonetheless. You used your senses to feel the aura around you and it protected you. By doing so you have taken your first step into the greater abilities of magic; and its techniques.

"But, I think one more thing is at hand for today. It is energy consuming but an important part of the sorcerer's training. Perhaps even the most important."

"Does it work like the last one?" questioned Leo.

"Yes, but this time we will use it to evoke the energy around you. By this, we create magic. Whether it is fire, water, earth, wind or whatever it need be, you can make it. That is magic!" Eldred stabbed his own spear into the ground.

"Now – feel the aura around you again. Feel it deeper and stronger than before."

Leo breathed deeply and closed his eyes tightly. He felt different this time but why? He could feel a spark set off in his mind, almost like something trying to escape. Then, he raised his hand, palm side up. He felt a tingling rush through his arm and into his hand. His hand began to feel warm and fresh.

Eldred watched in amazement as Leo raised his hand. He could fell the magic in Leo's body rush to his hand, trying to create something.

A sudden spark struck from his palm, and then another. Leo's eyes opened. Leo fell to his knees, breathing heavily and rapidly. Leo's eyes widened and then – he collapsed.

$$- 0 -$$

He opened his eyes. Leo's eyes strained as he looked around in the darkened room. He kicked the bed sheets off him and looked around, squinting both of his eyes painfully. A thundering headache echoed through him like a hollow pipe. Leo groaned, and dropped his body onto the bed.

It took a few minutes before the drumming in Leo's head stopped. He rubbed his head and his eyes, looking up. He was in the healing ward, yet again. Eldred stood above him.

"Good evening. You must spend less time in here, you know," said Eldred, smiling. Leo laughed, crossing his legs and sitting up.

"Too right – I guess I'm just not strong enough..." he said. Eldred shook his head.

"No, no. You're much stronger than I thought, actually. I never expected you to be able to use magic so, well, swiftly. You should be proud."

"I suppose," said Leo. Eldred sat down beside Leo, grasping his staff.

"You are an amazing person, Leo," said Eldred.

"Wha– me? No I'm not!" Leo exclaimed, embarrassed.

"Yes! Yes you are!" said Eldred, slightly louder. "You may

not think it, but I can see many things have happened in a short space of your lifetime. There's... there's a lot of suffering, is there not?"

"Yes," Leo said bluntly. "How do you know?"

"From your movement," said Eldred, standing up slowly, "and your focus. Emotions are easily seen on the outside. That is why a sorcerer hides them and does not use them. Magic and emotion do not mix. If they do, terrible things will happen. Like what happened at Yarnsdale...'

"So," began Leo, startled, "...that's what happens."

Eldred took his oak staff and prodded the bed covers back over Leo. "Yes, I'm afraid so. But, rest. Now is the best time to clear your mind." Eldred bowed slightly and left, flicking his hand and magically closing the door as he left.

− 0 −

Damn it, I can't sleep, thought Leo. Leo squirmed around in his bed, trying to get comfortable. It just wouldn't work. He grumbled angrily and sat up. *Stupid, stuffy bed.* He hated it when he couldn't sleep. He got so bored.

Leo stared around for a while, and then decided to try and sleep again. *Maybe if I clear my mind...* Wait a minute...

He pulled the covers off and knelt on the bed. He took a long look and then closed his eyes. Pitch black filled his view. He listened to his breathing, his chest rising and falling. As he breathed, he smelled something vaguely familiar then the smooth touch of his clothing became more important. Then, all these senses melted together and one thought slipped stealthily into his thoughts: *flame.*

Leo opened his eyes, slowly and carefully. He almost screamed. A small ball of flame, illuminating the bed, had appeared in his hand. He looked at it, amazed, and then threw it. He caught it in his other hand, but no pain was felt. He juggled the flame around, watching it swerve and spin. Then, he closed his hand and the flame disappeared.

A sudden excitement flooded through him. He had done it. He had made magic! He leapt out of bed and ran through the many corridors of the academy, not caring about the noise he made. He made his way to a steep staircase and hurried up as fast as he could muster.

"Eldred! Eldred! I've done it, I've done. . .'

"Eldred," someone spoke. Leo held his breath. Eldred's door was slightly ajar, just enough to hear inside. Leo, hesitantly, placed his back to the door and listened carefully.

"Why do you persist? This is not your place!" Eldred's voice roared. He heard his staff slam down strongly on the floor, and the wooden floor shook. Eldred then shouted in pain, and Leo could hear he had fallen to the floor.

"Why are you still in my head?" demanded Eldred.

"I *must* speak with him, please!" the voice sounded, almost pleaded, echoing throughout the room. Eldred's voice seemed taken aback.

"Leonard is none of your concern," replied Eldred, with a slight stutter. "You will not speak to him!"

There was a moment of insecurity and silence between the two people. Leo was, meanwhile, shocked to the bone – they were talking about him? What? Why? Leo pressed his ear harder now onto the door, almost making the door move inward even more than before. The voice resumed speaking.

"Can I not just see him?" it said, its voice now becoming softer, but still deep. "Just look in his eyes... "

"Be gone," finished Eldred. Then, the presence of the other person simply vanished from the room; almost as if it were never there. Leo slumped down on one of the walls outside of the oak chamber door. Someone was looking for him – who would want to look for him?

V

Preparations

Sunlight: perhaps the only thing that comforted Leo that dull morning. Everything was changing so fast... the excitement that had driven him yesterday was slowly vanishing. And now, someone was trying to see Leo and, obviously, not someone friendly. Leo growled angrily – why were the gods doing this to him?

He heard his door creak slightly. He looked up sharply – it was Sarah. She looked distraught and blushed slightly.

"I'm sorry," she said softly, "I should have knocked." She stepped out, closing the door behind her. Leo grumbled slightly at his depression and slammed his head in his palms.

What was he going to do? He just didn't know. Maybe if he... no, that wouldn't... but if he...

"Stupid complicated life," Leo groaned. He unfolded a set of his older robes and slowly changed into them. Maybe he should just tell Eldred he had heard him... wouldn't that make everything easier? But, there was something holding him back – almost like guilt. Why was he feeling guilty? He was going up to see Eldred; only to tell him about doing some magic. That was all. Yet, just thinking about it, it was the most stupid idea he had thought of. He could have just waited until the morning – but no! He had to go and see Eldred, didn't he! He could have done without this worry.

There was a knock on the door.

"Come in," said Leo, quietly. He first expected Sarah, or at least Eldred. He had to blink for a moment – it was Alex.

"Grumpy mood, aren't we?" said Alex. Leo nodded.

"It hasn't been the best of nights..." replied Leo.

"Hmm... why's that then?"

"I – I didn't sleep well," lied Leo. Alex looked at him sternly. He laughed slightly.

"Your bottom lip trembles when you lie, you know," he said.

"Really?" asked Leo in surprise, touching his lip.

"So... what's *really* wrong with you then?" asked Alex.

"It's nothing – just a slight shock, I suppose," answered Leo.

Alex stretched his arms slightly, and made his way to the door. "Just keep your head up. Besides, a man has to keep strong – even in the worst of times," he said. He left the room, closing the door as he went. Leo felt slightly comforted and smiled. Maybe Alex was right. If he just kept his chin up and pretended everything was fine, it would be

Oh, it had better be, thought Leo. He changed into his new robes and tied the cord tightly around his waist. Leo stood in deep thought for a moment. Then, he swiftly left his room, locking the door afterwards.

– 0 –

Leo stepped out onto the garden snow – but instead of the crispy snow there was a slippery rock tile on the ground. Caught unaware, he almost slipped over and stared surprisingly around. All the snow had melted: but only around the academy. Huh? That isn't right!

Leo looked and took a clear view of the countryside around him. Yup, the snow was still *over there* but not *here*. He sighed heavily and carefully made his way to the training circles in the field.

"There's always something happening wherever *I* am...' he said in annoyance. He made his way to the soggy grass field and the training circles on the stone ledge. He supposed these weird things would keep happening wherever he went. His life had changed completely these past few months and it wasn't going to stop. Not yet, anyway...

Leo heard the sound of footsteps behind him and turned to look. It was Sarah. Leo gave a small wave and brushed his hair out of his eyes. "Hi, Sarah."

"Hi to you too," she said, smiling. "So what's wrong with you today, then? Alex told me something was up."

"Well...' Leo started, "I dunno... confusion, anger – those sorts of things."

"In one night?" she said, unbelievably.

"Pretty much..." replied Leo. He sighed sadly. "I just hope things become clearer soon..."

"I hope so too," said Sarah, sitting down on the rock plate below to look at the clouds ahead. "My life hasn't been the

56

clearest either."

"I've never noticed," said Leo. "You're always so – so positive."

"Well, why not? Besides, it helps cheer people up. One person's smile can make another person's day a whole lot brighter," she explained. She placed her knees together and her hands placed gently on them. "I don't know if you know what I mean, but... "

"No, no – I get you," said Leo, smiling. "Your smile shows it – it's like a warm glow to me."

"Oh, thank you," Sarah said, blushing slightly. "I didn't know I did that." Both Sarah and Leo looked across to the academy as Alex ran towards them both.

"Hey there, Eldred wants to see us. He says it's important," he said bluntly. Sarah and Leo nodded and made their way to Eldred's quarters.

– 0 –

Eldred was sat on his large, crimson red sofa-chair with his legs propped-up on the desk. He quickly un-propped his legs and started twiddling his fingers. He was awfully nervous, for some reason; almost paranoid. He took a deep breath and calmed himself. He paced around the room slightly and then sat down again, taking another breath of air.

Leo, Alex and Sarah entered his chamber and an expression of relief was on his face. Alex leaned against the door, whereas Leo stood in the centre and Sarah sat on a small chair beside him. Eldred looked at them all with concern, like that of a father's look to his daughter, and then sat forward.

"Firstly, I just want to apologise to you, Leonard. I should have met you at the field but I had... a minor inconvenience," said Eldred. Leo nodded, but his mind still wondered over the night before; a minor inconvenience... *ha–ha, yeah right.*

"It doesn't matter," Leo said quickly, noticing his mind drifting off to another world.

"Anyway," continued Eldred, "I have an important task for you all to complete. It will take some time but it will prove its use to us all."

"What's the job?" asked Alex, formally.

"I need the three of you to research a powerful artefact known by the name of the *Soul Light*. I am, unfortunately, too pre-occupied to go myself. I know where I would go, though: the Loremaster's Tower. A friend of mine, Archimedes, will help you. He is a master of thought and knowledge and hopefully will find the answers I require."

"Where about is the tower?" asked Sarah.

"About 50 miles north-east of here," answered Eldred.

"Wh – 50 miles?" spurted Alex in surprise. Eldred laughed.

"Yes, Alex, 50 miles. It shouldn't take you too long to travel there – two, perhaps three, days of hustled walk. That is pre-suming you travel through the Greatwood Split rather than through the woods themselves. Anyway, do you wish to go or am I going to have to move these creaky knees of mine?" questioned Eldred. The three looked at each other, as if men-tally speaking to each other, and then turned to Eldred. Sarah nodded confidently, whereas Alex simply nodded once and looked rather disgruntled about walking. Leo, however, took a few seconds to make a reaction. His mind clicked with sudden worried thoughts, but he knew he was better off doing as Eldred said. He nodded.

"Ah, very good, very good. You had best be leaving to-morrow – once the cold weather has past. Good day," finished Eldred. He stood up and made his way to a grand oak cup-board and surveyed its contents. Leo waited for both Sarah and Alex to leave first, pretending to do the same, and then turned to Eldred.

"Um... Eldred, if you don't mind – could I ask you some-thing?" he asked nervously, biting his bottom lip slightly. Eldred turned to face Leo.

"Why certainly, Leo, what seems to be the problem?" he asked comfortingly.

"It's just – I don't think I want to go off with the others. I want to stay here and practise my magic," explained Leo.

"Leo, Leo, Leo... you will have plenty of time to spend on developing your rudimentary magic; you have your entire life ahead of you. But this is where we exchange our services: I give to you training, advice and magic. Now, you must return the favour by researching this object."

"But this thing, this *Soul Light*, what significance is it to me?"

asked Leo, getting bitter.

"The world would be such a better place if we all gave, rather than wanted," complained Eldred. "Trust me, Leo. This object will help you more than you will believe. Just help me and I will help you." Leo grunted to himself, and then nodded reluctantly. Eldred smiled slightly.

"Don't be too disappointed, Leo. Besides, adventure is the one word that can inspire all. Take the opportunity to learn about the world around you and see new places," said Eldred. He gestured towards the door and pulled out a quill from his ink pot and began scribbling on a stained piece of parchment. Leo opened the door and left, slowly making his way down the stairs.

It wasn't so bad, he supposed. He never really travelled much in his life – plus he would be able to learn a lot about the outside world. And Eldred was right after all, it would just be an adventure. Not the most exciting one, but...

– 0 –

There seemed to be an uneasy silence as the afternoon past – the breath before the plunge. It seemed everyone was doing something to prepare themselves (except Eldred, who remained in his quarters). Alex, who had seemed to vanish that afternoon, simply said that he needed time to himself. Leo, on the other hand, sat in meditation in the fields of grass and practised his developing magic.

Surprisingly, things were becoming clearer. In only a few days he had made many different things; fire, wind and water. It was as if his mind had known all along – but just couldn't access it. Ironic, really: Leo had thought so anyway. All this power locked away and unable to use it? Nevertheless, Leo remained slightly proud of his accomplishments and did his best to hide his satisfied grin from Eldred.

The fields outdoors had a cooling ice breeze as night approached. Leo had looked forward to a cool down and paced to his usual training spot. He removed the shirt of his robes and sat down to take in the breeze. The feeling was great as it swept along his chest and sent a shuddering chill down his spine.

That's better, thought Leo calmly. DANGER! Leo swiped his

59

hand up by his cheek and caught something – thin and pointed at the end. He opened his left eye and glimpsed at the red-feathered, oak arrow and the thin drop of dark blood at its steel point. He placed the arrow on the ground and jumped up, surveying the area. Assassins? Archers? Invaders? Leo looked around fearfully and then saw someone coming up the hill. He focused his mind and, in a few seconds time margical whips of air slashed around him creating a thin shield for his body. He opened his eyes and clenched his fists tightly, ready to fight.

Yet Leo's eyes widened at this person. For t'was no invader, no assassin nor any foe to be reckoned with – it was Sarah. She held a longbow in both her hands and a quiver was clipped by her hip. She then hurried over to Leo, with a look of deep grief upon her tender face.

"Leo, I'm so sorry! I – I didn't realise you were there," she said quickly, kneeling beside him.

"No, no – it's fine," Leo replied calmly, simply wiping away the small bubble of blood from the cut. It was his fault really. He then noticed the wooden board a few feet away from him with arrows deeply impaled into them.

"Typical, really..." said Leo, raising his eyebrows at his own ignorance.

"Yeah... typical that boys are all as blind as bats," laughed Sarah. Leo turned to face her as she stood up.

"Hmm, you can't really talk, can you? Almost killed me with an arrow!" he said, grinning. They both laughed at each other and Leo moved out of the way of Sarah's position as she began drawing an arrow from her quiver.

"Have you been doing archery for long, then?" asked Leo, sitting on the damp grass whilst tightening his robe.

"Since I came here – Eldred showed me how and I liked it," she replied, aiming carefully at the target.

"Any good?" he asked. Sarah then released the arrow, sending it flying straight into the bullseye.

"Don't really know," said Sarah, brushing her hair back and winking. Leo simply laughed to himself and continued to watch. He wasn't sure how long he stayed there watching – something just grasped him. It could have easily been her concentration or epic skill, but, he simply stared at her as she took each careful shot.

– 0 –

The day had drawn dark when Leo entered the academy after watching Sarah. All he really cared about now was getting some well-deserved sleep before leaving. God, he wished he had more time. Then again, that's life for you.

Leo slowly made his way through the corridors, rubbing his weary eyes and yawning wildly. To his surprise, however, he found Eldred scuttling around the corridors looking desperately around. A look of relief flourished his face when he saw a tired Leo making his way to his room.

"Leo! I have something important for you," said Eldred, hurrying towards him.

"Eh?" Leo grunted half-asleep. Eldred looked annoyingly at Leo and stepped back away from him.

"What is it?" asked Leo, his eyes thinning. A sudden gush of freezing cold water poured down onto the entirety of Leo's clothes. A colossal shiver spread through his whole body – invigorating his nerves and muscles. Leo spat out some water from his mouth. Eldred, on the other hand, merely smiled and asked: "Awake now?"

The two made their way to Eldred's chambers, where Eldred sat in his usual armchair behind the desk and Leo simply stood, waiting for whatever he was to be told. Eldred composed himself and then leaned forward placing his hands together and resting his elbows on the cluttered desk of parchment and ink. He also clicked his fingers, and the drenched clothing that Leo wore, suddenly lost all moisture and became warm again.

"I have some things in here for your journey tomorrow," said Eldred, now standing up and walking to a peculiar large oak cupboard with gold trimming.

"Something for me?" asked Leo in surprise. Then again it wasn't the first time Eldred had surprised him with a gift. Leo stood next to him as Eldred peered through the cupboard and, to Leo's surprise, the inside space was huge; it was almost another room completely. Strange mechanisms were inside clicking; rotating planets on a large spindle; large piles of dusty parchment; exotic weapons and armour; a strange, encrypted

61

amulet lay on the floor and then a great pile of many different things. Eldred, however, pushed back the piles of parchment for almost a minute before reaching a small, thin glass case. Leo tried to see what was inside but couldn't make out what it was.

"Now," began Eldred, "this is something you will need and it's very important for your protection, Leo." He wiped clean the dust and then carefully slid the base of the case out. Then, the object was revealed.

"A... a stick?" Leo said, doings his best to hold back the laughter.

"A stick? This is no stick, Leo; this is a much more fascinating thing. This is a wand!" said Eldred excitedly. However, the excitement from Leo he had expected wasn't quite there...

"But, Eldred, I'm a sorcerer; not a demimage. I don't need this," said Leo, however secretly admiring the intricate design of the wand: golden flames whirling around the wand like a whirlwind.

"I suppose I should have told you about this before you left, I seem to have left it too late," sighed Eldred, who left the cupboard open and sat down at his desk again. He placed the wand down on the desk and Leo stood and listened.

"For over 7,000 years the sorcerers were the keepers of lore and the binders of peace. We made Asgarth a great realm and continent, one without war or treachery. Our magical gifts resolved problems before they could start and no–one dared to cross paths against law and good. But then, the great sorcerer known as Merlin began to pity the people of the normal world. There is magic in everyone, you see, Leo, and they need only the drive, the extra *push* to find it.

"So, Merlin the Great worked long and hard upon finding the key to allowing all to use magic. He found it. Dragon blood – such a powerful liquid. As you know, it is believed that sorcerers were offspring from the many generations of draconic families, as it is this blood that is needed for the magic we use. Merlin the Great sent many great forces on the largest expedition known in the history of mankind itself. Hundreds, perhaps thousands, of dragons were slain. Their blood fused into items to evoke magic. You know what I am talking about, of course. Wands and staffs: objects now permanently attached to a demimage's key equipment."

"So, what happened to them? I mean, I never knew there was

a difference between a sorcerer and demimage before!" claimed Leo.

"As the millenniums passed, more and more demimages were born. It had become a great profession and one with many uses. Soon, the demimages formed academies and became well-known to royals and nobles. The sorcerers had lost their position in authority and could not even teach their skills to others. This led to what is known as the Great Revolt, almost 900 years ago."

"What happened?"

"Sorcerers from all over the continent took a stand against the powerful and the nobles. It was an understandable thing, for we had been the keepers and councillors of the land for so long, and we did not want to be replaced by demimages. Ironically, the pity of Merlin became our downfall. For the first offensive move was made not by us, but by the demimages, thanks to the King."

"The – they attacked?" said Leo, in surprise. Eldred nodded.

"The King believed that eventually the sorcerer line would die, and that an army of demimages of tens of thousands would be much more suitable. So, thousands of sorcerers were slaughtered; we did not take this lightly, but stood our ground and took down many of our enemy, too. But it did not end there. We were hunted down, Leo. Great numbers of assassins were hired to hunt down sorcerer leaders or the wise. Only a few survivors remained." In recognition, Leo began to stare down at the wand he held. It had seemed to become an object of evil – a tool that murdered thousands.

"What does it have to do with this wand, though?" asked Leo.

"It is a tool that can be used to bluff," replied Eldred.

"So, I should use it as a disguise?"

"Exactly!" exclaimed Eldred, clapping his hands. "I hope you understand the reason now, too. The sorcerers became hated and if it were to be discovered that some remain, the hunters and assassins could easily return."

Eldred stood up and shuffled his way to the cupboard again. Leo slid the wand neatly into the inside of his shirt and then looked back over to Eldred, who was now causing a large racket. Suddenly, a long black pole slowly appeared; then a dark red feather (where the blade joined the shaft) and finally a strange blade: somewhat like a metallic fang. Eldred handed it to Leo, who took it and ran his hand along the blade and shaft. The blade felt slightly coarse to the touch and had no metallic gleam.

"Strange blade isn't it?" said Eldred, curiously. Leo nodded. "Where did you get it from?" he asked.

"It was a gift from a friend. I have never used it, however. I noticed it more when you arrived, though, so I thought it would be a reasonable gift. Every sorcerer needs his weapon."

"Thank you," replied Leo. Eldred closed the creaking cupboard doors and then hustled Leo out.

"Get a good night's rest, you'll need it for the journey," he explained. Leo agreed and exited, still admiring the spear. Eldred muttered afterwards: "For your sake, put it to good use. . ."

– 0 –

With the morning sun's rise, Leo, Sarah and Alex were already waiting to make a move to the Loremaster's Tower. The three were sat patiently, waiting for the humble words of Eldred to set them off, but he had not yet appeared to greet and send them off.

Leo had decided to wear the exotic robes that Eldred had given him, believing it to be a symbol of recognition. He held Eldred's spear in one hand, pointing downward, and with his other hand he simply made and played with small sparks of magic.

Sarah, meanwhile, wore a buttoned, amber shirt that was decorated with golden strips of silk. She then had a long, thin, blood–red coloured skirt. However, the beauty of the clothing and her face sneakily disguised the quiver of arrows resting on her back. The yew longbow, however, was held with both her hands as she sat upon a small rock and twiddled the string to strengthen it.

Finally, Alex wore a dark brown shirt and long, saggy black trousers. His boots were dark and he wore fingerless leather gloves. Sheathed on his right hip was a longsword, yet Leo knew that Alex would hardly find use for such a thing – he was too much of a pyromaniac.

The silence lasted another few minutes before Eldred came, stumbling along half-asleep and in some shabby robes.

"Awful night," he laughed. He rummaged through his pouch as the three watched anxiously. He pulled out a small bronze device. A blade atop it spun and then pointed diagonally from them. He then handed the device to Sarah, who placed it in her dress' skirt.

"What is that?" asked Leo, who had no idea what those tools were.

"This is a compass," explained Sarah, "but not a normal one. It always points towards the tower, so we won't get lost. Then, it can be set automatically back to the Academy."

"A very intriguing tool," smiled Eldred. "Master Alim produced it himself; it's used widely by many rich folk." Eldred then took a second item, from his sleeve this time, and handed it to Alex. Leo took a closer look— oh, it was a feather... what?

"Err... I suppose this is another ingenious mechanism?" Leo presumed. Eldred nodded.

"Of course, this feather easily transmutes into as many tents as you might need to camp for. Should be grateful too, otherwise I'll make you carry a nice burdensome tent around for days on end." Eldred simply smiled as Leo laughed awkwardly, scratching the back of his head.

"Well, I suppose you should begin travelling now," said Eldred. "Sarah – make sure you're careful and do watch your aim. Alex, try not to set fire to too many things this time. And Leo, do not take my warning lightly – keep your emotions controlled. Don't lose focus. That is all I have to say." The group all nodded and began to turn.

"Oh, and also, don't be too long. It does get awfully lonely in the academy," he added. They all smiled and Sarah waved as they left Eldred, who returned to the academy. Leo only had his thoughts on what he had been told.

Keep your emotions under control... that one he *had* to remember – for everyone's sake. Don't want Alex running around on fire now, do we? Wait, Alex does that normally anyway – never mind.

VI

The Ominous Warning

"Are we *there* yet?" Those four words simply echoed and echoed between Leo and Alex, only to be answered with a peeved remark of 'no' from Sarah. This journey... it was just... it was just taking so damn long!

The three had been walking for two whole days, more of a forced march when it was with Sarah. Leo and Alex would mumble together that women were too demanding... far too demanding. Leo was beginning to regret the excitement of travelling – the blisters on his feet agreed too.

"Oh stop being such cry-babies you two," said Sarah, watching the compass in her palm as it slowly pointed in the tower's direction.

"Well, *you* don't have to live with blistering feet now, do you?" argued Leo, with Alex nodding in agreement. Sarah simply spun her head away with a 'humpf' and continued walking. Alex rolled his eyes upwards and he and Leo followed as ordered.

"Anyway, I haven't seen much of you at the academy since I've been here, Alex," said Leo. "What do you do, anyway?"

"Me? I simply practise on my own natural abilities," answered Alex.

"So... you play with fire?"

"Ha, I suppose you could say that," laughed Alex, conjuring a small flame on his fingertip. "But practise makes perfect."

"Trust me, Leo, don't make him mad," said Sarah ahead of them. "You don't want to see him when he's mad."

"Oh, you're talking to us now are you?" asked Leo. Sarah simply stuck her tongue out at him and they shared a smile afterwards.

"Do you reckon we will reach the tower by tomorrow?" asked Alex, fed up with the pacing of his feet over and over and over...

"Might even make it tonight, we've made quite a distant in two days. According to the dial we only have 10 miles to go now."

"That's the best news I've heard all day," smiled Leo, pulling out his spear and spinning it around.

"Leo, it's the *only* news you've heard all day, you numb-nut," Sarah finished. She suddenly stopped in her path, her voice making a small, taken-a-back sound. Leo also felt something – a change in the air. Alex stopped beside Sarah and looked around.

"What is it?" he asked in concern, his eyes narrowed and surveying around.

"I saw something – like a wisp of shadow," she answered. She gently raised her hand to her quiver, ready to draw an arrow. Leo took a moment of quiet calm – then turned around. A hooded figure stood a few feet away on the hills they travelled along. He wore long, black robes with silver chains hanging from the cloak's hood. The large hood submerged his face threateningly in darkness. No feature of his face could be seen and his body simply stood neutrally, both arms to his sides with his palms cupped towards him.

"Who are you?" Leo demanded, raising his spear. The figure ignored the spear and took a step forward.

"You do not wish to threaten me," a male, yet emotionless voice was heard from the figure. "You threaten yourself by searching for it."

"What is he talking about?" Sarah whispered to Leo. Leo lowered his spear and also took a cautious step forward.

"Do not look for it," the figure demanded. "Such a thing belongs to me – if I do not find it I will surely suffer for all eternity."

"We do not look for it, only information," said Alex, realising what the figure was talking about. There was a moment's uneasy hush.

"You should not even know about it," the ominous figure continued, now looking down at the ground. "No one should know it – the plan should have held. Did they fail?"

"What? Who are they?" asked Leo.

"They do not concern you. You should not know – something went wrong," the figure said, still in an emotionless tone. The figure then raised its head, as if to look in Leo's eyes. "Do not continue this. You will lose too much. Continue this and I shall kill you all. Something has gone wrong." The last sentence echoed from his voice, chilling the three like a ghost. The figure then became shrouded in black air – the air passed and nothing remained. Only a swirl of dust moved from where he once stood.

"So... what the hell was that about?" asked Alex angrily. Leo turned to him and Sarah, simply staring at the ground.

"How am I supposed to know? The weird thing didn't make any sense," he said.

"Still...' said Sarah, "when we next see Eldred, we should tell him. That was too strange to ignore." Alex and Leo nodded, but Leo was still concerned that the figure had threatened them with death. What *did* Eldred want with this 'Soul Light', anyway?

This had better be worth it, thought Leo. They stood together for a moment, and then continued on their way. It had been the third day of travel, and already something was going badly for them. Leo angrily muttered in quiet: "Why does everything bad happen to me?"

– 0 –

Night filled the sky and the full moon shone its silver light onto the range of hills across the land. The sky was cloudless and small gold stars glinted in random constellation. The land had become darker and Leo badly needed to sleep.

"Why are we still going?" he said drearily. "Why don't we just stop here?"

"Because... if we make it to the tower we can sleep in beds and bathe – wouldn't you prefer that?" replied Sarah, who wasn't looking too keen at the ground below her feet. Who would want to sleep in mud, anyway?

Sarah suddenly gave a quiet 'yip' as she looked down the hillside, where she stood. Leo and Alex hurried to her side quickly. A huge, marble range of towers rested at the bottom of the steep hill. The moonlight seemed to reflect off its surface, lighting it with a peculiar silver glow. The building started off like a huge square at the bottom and split off into many towers as it reached higher and higher into the sky. They had made it in just three days – good praise for Sarah was a must.

The three hurried down the hill together to the iron gates of the tower, where a simply dressed man in silk robes stood. The man, slightly surprised at the late arrivals, quickly neatened his robes as they approached.

"Hello there, young ones. What brings you to the Loremaster's Tower?" the gatekeeper asked kindly. The three stood for a moment, unsure who would speak first. Leo was, unfortunately, nudged forward nervously to end the silence.

"We... we wish to use the libraries of the tower. Oh, and a place to rest if – if you have room," said Leo, with jittery, nervous voice. The gatekeeper smiled at his feeble speech and then made a signal with his hand behind him. A few more robed men appeared and heaved open the iron gates.

"I'm afraid the libraries are closed after hours. You will have to wait until the morning," explained the gatekeeper, who guided them through long marble halls. Many people rushed past – many robed and some others in royal clothing.

"Understandable," said Alex.

"For now, you will have to be in the dormitories until the morning, I presume two dorms? One for the fine lady and the other for you two?" asked the gatekeeper. Alex and Leo looked at each other and both grudgingly sighed. Sarah simply smiled and nodded.

It took a few minutes to reach the dormitories, even though they were on the ground floor of the tower. This place was just huge! The gatekeeper found two dorms, both next to each other, and handed them each keys from a locked cabinet near the doors. He then bowed to them and departed back to his gating duties. Sarah unlocked her door, bid them a goodnight and entered, locking the door behind her.

Leo followed Alex into the room – and what a room it was! Dark red curtains with gold lace spanned the window, beds of fine crafted wood with beautiful linen sheets stood in the room, large oak dressers were lined against the wall, through another door was a large bath linked with large gold pipes, followed by many sinks and toilets.

And Leo thought he was lucky at Eldred's... these loremasters sure knew how to live life in style. Leo collapsed onto his bed and felt his eyelids droop. He knew there was a busy day ahead, but the sheets just felt so nice. Just a little nap...

– 0 –

Leo was abruptly awoken by the shaking of his entire body. He quickly opened his eyes drearily and saw Sarah by his side, moving his shoulder.

"Come on, Leo, wake up!" she then shouted.

"Ugh... just another hour...' Leo groaned, trying to pull the sheets over. Sarah stood up and heaved the covers off him.

"Look, it's almost noon already, so get up!" she said. Leo pulled himself up and rubbed his sleepy eyes of their tiresome manner. Sarah couldn't help but giggle.

"It's hard to believe you're supposed to be a sorcerer, sometimes," she laughed. Leo grimaced and stood up, scratching his head.

"I'm still learning..." he said coarsely, "plus I'm still human!" Leo stood up and concentrated on refreshing himself. He waved his hand down his body and with magic felt his pores feel clearer and healthier, as if they had been cleaned by water.

"Oh... so Mr. Sorcerer is starting to do magic now, is he?" smiled Sarah. Leo rolled his eyes and then walked out with her. Leo followed Sarah, who seemed to know where she was going, and they started ascending a large, spiral stone staircase. After a painful course upward, they reached a large circular room that was filled with shelves of all kinds of books. It seemed everything you ever wanted to know was in here. His eyes even spotted a book called *Sorcerers: The Betrayers of Asgarth* and another called *Sorcerers: Living Demons!* Leo grimaced at these books, remembering what Eldred had told them of the mass slaughter of sorcerers many years ago. Sarah pulled him over to Alex, who, unlike the image he had first had of Alex, was pouring over many books.

"Any luck on the Soul Light?" asked Leo. Alex shook his head.

"Nothing so far, but I've only been going for an hour," he replied.

Only? thought Leo. Leo looked around at the books about him: *Ancient Artefacts of Asgarth, A Timeline of Creations* and other books flooded along a whole row of bookshelves. Leo sighed — off to work...

— 0 —

Leo didn't know how long he had been in the library, and it was likely neither Sarah nor Alex did. The evening had almost passed and the library would soon close. They had poured

70

through hundreds of books, skimming the details and reading through – but there was nothing. Absolutely nothing about any Soul Light. If this had been a joke, Leo wouldn't feel so bad. But this seemed important to Eldred; Leo couldn't help but feel a sense of failure. Then again, they still had time.

Leo, feeling more invigorated to find out what the blasted thing was, decided to take his chances and ask the librarians. He walked up to one, an old woman with white hair, who was dealing with another sage and then turned to Leo afterwards.

"Hello, is there a problem?" she said, looking at him through half-moon spectacles.

"Yes," he pointed towards Sarah and Alex, who were both looking very depressed, "we have been looking for a certain artefact, but haven't had much luck. It's called the Soul Light – do you have any ideas about it?"

The women looked slightly shocked but then quickly composed herself. "I'm sorry, I've never heard of such a thing," she said. "I would just keep looking I'm afraid." She then walked along to a bell and rang it loudly around the room.

"The libraries are now closing! Please make your way down the stairs!" she exclaimed. Leo waited for Sarah and Alex whilst watching the many people going down the stairs.

"What's wrong?" asked Sarah, concerned by the expression on his face.

"They're hiding it from us," Leo replied, watching the female librarian he had just spoken to.

"What? Why?" said Alex, quickly.

"Give me time, I'll find out. Just distract her!" he quickly whispered as she approached them. Leo moved to the side and Sarah quickly stepped forward to the librarian.

"Excuse me," said Sarah, in a very girlish and posh form. "Will the library be open earlier tomorrow, being a Saturday?"

Leo took his chance – he snuck out of the view of the librarian and hid behind a book case near the other end of the library. He could now only hear muttered conversation. He watched as the two left, Sarah winking to him cutely as she passed down the stairs and Alex simply taking a quick glimpse (Leo presumed that was his way of mentally saying 'good luck').

The librarian walked passively for a bit around the library then walked down the stairs quickly. Leo followed closely, down the stairs, hiding occasionally from view. The corridors were quite empty now and he had to hide only a view times because of other people. Leo continued to track along her footsteps, listening carefully to movement and any minute sound.

It took a while for the librarian to stop – it seemed she had been looking for someone. A much older, and wiser looking man stood in the corridors. She then muttered something to him and rushed him along more corridors. Leo quickly followed, having trouble to keep up with them whilst being stealthy. They finally stopped in a room in the corner of two adjoining corridors. The door was made of very fine, polished oak and had a gold leaf-design painted on the door. There was a sign nailed to the door, with gold letters and a gold frame. Leo took a closer look, tightening his eyes to focus on the letters: *The Royal Library*. That might explain a lot of the problems they were having; if there was to be any information on the Soul Light, it would be *here*.

The problem, however, was that these two librarians were standing in the way. He edged closer and pressed his body into a small alcove along the corridor and listened in on their conversation.

"... I'm telling you," the female librarian said, "they knew about it! How on earth did they know about it?"

"Yes," the other replied, with a deep voice, "but *we* shouldn't know about it either! It's the king's personal library! He would have us hanged if he found out!"

"Still this is worrying me... ' she continued. She quickly pulled out a key and unlocked the royal library's doors and ushered the other librarian in, saying: "In case anyone else hears." Leo took his chances; he peered around a few corners to check for other people and then shifted his body to the door. He carefully placed his ear to the door and listened to the muffled voices inside.

"We can't take them in!" a male voice said, "because that means that the king will know that we know about it too! The tower would have to be closed!"

"So, you think we should just – just *leave them?*"

"We don't have any choice. Besides, there's nothing they will find out about it and there's no way they can get into the royal library. Now just forget about the incident. I'm sure they will too when they don't find out about it."

"But Archimedes..."

"No buts!" The final voice shouted, and Leo felt something move the door he was listening into. He quickly jumped back as the door swung wide open. Leo's heartbeat began to rush – he was trapped. If they caught him listening in – oh God, who knows what would happen? Leo saw the footsteps move out of the room. He needed something; *anything*. Leo looked around desperately, and then saw one of the pair of feet turn to the other. They began talking, but Leo wasn't listening.

Leo then remembered his training – keep calm. He took a few deep breaths and then concentrated.

A *distraction*, he thought, *a sound, anything*. He opened his eyes and raised his hand up in a clenched fist. He had his eyes tightly closed and then... he released his grip suddenly, spreading his fingers wide. BANG! The two librarians spun towards the opposite corridor and took several steps forward. Leo lunged himself into the royal library and hid behind a pile of dusty books that lay scattered. The door was then closed and locked, as one librarian shouted: "Quick! Lock it! We need to find out what that was!" There was a scuttle of footsteps and then... silence.

Leo took a deep, long rest from the excitement. He'd got in! *I think I'm getting to grip with this magic...*

The room was dark and musty, which didn't help for a room only slightly larger than a broom cupboard. It was simply circular, with one bookcase spanning the entirety of the room. Books had been scattered on the floor (possibly the king's doing) and dust had seemed to have built up like pyramids over time.

Leo found a lamp and removed the case. He spent some time conjuring a flame, with the wick fluttering and producing small puffs of black smoke. It eventually lit and illuminated the room. Leo raised the lantern and scanned along the bookcase, blowing away dust to read the titles of the books. Some were in forms of different languages whereas others were falling apart, page by page. Leo finally found the book. He placed the lantern on the pile of mounting books on the floor and pulled the book out. It was a very thin book, just a few pages or so. After blowing and wiping away the dust its title was revealed: *Account of the Soul Light, Origin and Purpose*. Leo smiled happily to himself pleased

73

with his success and, without hesitation, opened it up. The writing was handwritten and wavy, some letters were detailed differently to normal – this was obviously a very old text. Not impossible to understand, however. Leo read through:

For the King of Asgarth's eyes only: be sinned if not that person (Leo winced at the thought, but continued).

The Soul Light, its location I shall not reveal, is hidden in a deep place beyond any race's reach. It is an item of purity and has held as a seal for a long time. Yet I fear the worst.

Its power is beyond that of any mundane item, for it holds the power to hold off those who wish to attack us. That is what makes it an effective seal. It keeps the evil at bay and has since secured Asgarth of hell's creation.

It is unlikely that it can be removed from its position. It has been guarded by magic and a terrible guardian protects it. The guardian was hired in my time and has been commanded to find a greater guardian should it be nearing death. However, the guardian is a powerful one and should not be crossed under any circumstance. It no longer recognises friend from foe.

If it goes, you will know, my lord. Not at first instance but in a most drastic way that you must constantly be prepared for. The Soul Light is needed to protect the people and if taken must be used for the greater good. If it is not for good, than I foresee a darker age towards the people of Asgarth. Control is possible with this tool – that is all I will say. Do not allow this to happen, your majesty.

I fear for the future, may these words offer you wisdom to be passed through the generations.

Lord Dragir

Leo finished reading the text – it seemed this person had huge handwriting to have filled what had been three pages. At least he had found the information – he almost hid the book under his cloak, when he realised the librarians would notice a book missing. He looked around and found some old parchment as well as a quill and inkpot. He may as well copy it; at least it would be a little less suspicious. . .

AAHHHH! Leo's head turned suddenly towards the door. A scream –this wasn't good; right outside the door too. He had to get out. He threw away the parchment and grabbed the book. He moved back slightly, and then slammed his foot into the door.

"Oww!" he shouted angrily. He took a moment to compose himself, then rammed his whole body and effort into the door, smashing the lock and landing on the ground. He almost screamed himself when he looked to his side. A body – the librarian's body from the tower! He could hardly bear to see her body – burnt and mutilated. It was hard to distinguish anything on her – only the half-moon spectacles identified her.

Leo couldn't wait around here: he had to get out and run. He quickly closed the door, which was now hanging off its hinge, and ran out to the corridor. There was a glimpse of many people rushing to the scene, but none had seen him. He continued through the corridors and then finally made it to his dormitory. Sarah and Alex were already walking towards the incident.

"DON'T GO THERE!" Leo yelled uncontrollably. Alex caught him as Leo almost sped past them.

"Leo, slow down! What's going on?" Alex asked firmly. Leo's breathing was heavy, but managed to utter the words needed.

"Got... the info... someone's dead... don't know... what happened..."

"Someone's been killed?" Sarah asked worryingly. Leo nodded, and then pulled out the book from under his arm.

"Everything we need is in here. We have to leave..." explained Leo.

"What – you got it! So why leave?" said Sarah. Leo took a moment to reply and then swallowed; his breath was still quite heavy.

"That is supposed to be me dead... I just know it. It's that person we met before we got here – I just know it!" Leo exclaimed. Sarah and Alex agreed and they quickly entered their rooms, grabbing their gear and Sarah put the book in her leather backpack.

"Let's get out of here," Leo shouted, picking up his spear. The floor suddenly shook and dust fell from the ceiling.

"Wh– what the hell was that?"; Alex suddenly shouted, looking up at the ceiling. RUMBLE. Another shake. None of them said anything – but the speed of their running said

75

enough. RUMBLE. The tower shook again. They ran back to the entrance hall. The iron gates were open and unguarded, but outside there must have been more than a hundred people gazing up at the tower. The darkening night was aglow with flames upon the highest towers that burned savagely with huge flames. The libraries were burning! Leo knew that they had to move away – if not for his own sake but for the people in the tower.

"C'mon," Leo quickly said and Sarah and Alex followed suit. There was no time to lose.

– 0 –

The three ran for quite some time, jogging south from the Tower. Even from that distance, the raging flames could be seen. Although they had died down, it seemed whatever fury had caused them was still burning strong. Leo didn't like any of this – he knew whole-heartedly that this was because of the Soul Light. He hated having the guilt of something happening upon him – it was too much tension.

"What do you suppose we do?" asked Leo, stopping from jogging and halted.

"Well, if you're right, we have to get to Eldred," said Alex. "I just hope you were wrong."

"Unlikely," said Sarah, "that person we met said we shouldn't know about the Soul Light..."

"How does Eldred know about it?" Leo cut in. Sarah nodded. Alex sat himself on the thin grass, and also opened up his water–skin.

"This goes deeper than we realise," he said, then taking a large drink of water. "Really, we shouldn't be so nosy. This is Eldred's business. We just deliver the information." Leo agreed. They just had to tell Eldred what had happened – and that would be that.

Leo then felt something – the wind had seemed to change direction. He quickly stood up, looking at a small swirling of wind a few feet away.

"Someone's coming," he said. Sarah and Alex also jumped up, noticing the swirling winds.

"And it's not friendly..." Leo finished, drawing his spear.

Sarah notched an arrow into her bow, while Alex simply stood and waited.

The swirling winds began to turn purple, then into an inky meld of black. The winds dipped and then rose into the air for a moment, then vanished – revealing a cloaked figure; it was the person from yesterday!

"You. . .' Leo muttered angrily. The figure made no movement, but it could be felt that a smile had come across his concealed face.

"Often, a 'you' has a name," he sneered.

"Good point," Alex concurred. "So what is your name?"

"Only people have names." Around the figure, further dark clouds of misty wind swirled around, first five – then ten. . . and then Leo lost count. More and more just kept appearing, again and again. They all faded down simultaneously to reveal men – shaggy and scruffy. Each had a blade drawn, some rusty or broken, and each sneered happily with laughing grunts.

"These people, however, do have names," the figure continued. "Each one has their own, but I do prefer to give them a group name. . . perhaps bandits would be a fine choice, don't you agree?"

"Trust a stinking coward to . . . "

"Watch your tongue!" the figure snapped in before Leo. "Your ignorance astounds me. There I was, burning down the tower before your very eyes with the smallest of movements. Yet you stand here, unafraid, and have the nerve to insult me."

"There are worse things than death," Leo said bravely, understanding the figure's power. The figure said nothing, but instead surveyed Leo for a moment from beneath his hood.

"I understand now. . . you think you have suffered worse than death – but what you have experienced is of feeble mind and utterly pathetic devotion. What you once imagined was a dream, and dreams so easily crack under pressure. . .

"I told you, you knew too much. Yet the three of you continued and went against my very words. Now, you know far, far too much. It comes to an end, my friends. You lives must cease now and forever."

VII

An Unforgettable Curse

Leo looked around observing all of the ill-content men surrounding him, Sarah and Alex. As he turned back round to face their leader – he vanished in the swirling black cloud he once formed from. There was a moment's pause, as the wind swept across them, and then Leo slowly lifted his spear.

"Suggestions?" Leo asked to Alex and Sarah, yet not leaving his concentration on the bandits.

"Fire," Alex quickly said.

"Fire?" asked Leo, in surprise.

"Make me a flame, *now!*" Alex demanded. Leo raised his palm and then felt the rushing, burning sensation flow from his heart, through his arm and then rushing together in his palm. There was some pain – then a flame burst forth as a small, golden ember. A smile crossed Alex's face, and the flame was pulled away from Leo and became a huge, length of fire spiralling from each of his hands. Sarah, meanwhile, simply raised her bow slightly and gently brushed her fingers along the feathers of her arrows.

"I guess we're left with no choice…" Leo whispered. In a sudden rush of speed, Sarah unleashed her arrow and fired, slamming into the chest of the nearest bandit. The others looked down, startled and surprised, and then each ran upon them with blooded and rusting longswords drawn.

Leo readied his spear as they came toward him, but first sent a beam of energy from the tips of his opposite hand that set alight one of the bandits. Sarah took a second shot and pierced the leg of another making him fall onto the ground. Alex manipulated the fire he controlled and like a huge funnel, engulfed two of the bandits: when the flames returned to his hand, there was nothing but ash.

The remaining bandits, regardless of their fallen comrades, continued the charge, each with a manic grin across their faces. One took a swing at Leo, but Leo quickly ducked and sliced the spear through the bandit's heart. The swarm of bandits were, rather than attacking all three of them, surrounding Leo. Leo had to frantically spin around, using his spear to hold them off. When one tried to go for the killing strike, Leo would skilfully avoid the attack and pierce their heart.

Both Alex's and Sarah's attacks had slowed – they couldn't risk hurting Leo. Instead, they picked off the group one-by-one to help the tiring Leo.

But before anyone could react, a bandit sneered with rage and smashed down onto Leo's head with the butt of his longsword, making him fall to the ground on all-fours.

"Leo!" Alex shouted, he went to shoot the flame at the bandit above Leo, but it was too late. The bandit plunged down fiercely with sharp iron through Leo's back and out of his stomach, splattering blood over the grass. Leo looked up at Alex and Sarah, realizing what he had left them to...

This was his fault; his entire fault. He felt the distasteful blood rise to his mouth and felt it drip along his cheek, cooling as it ran like cold water down glass. He went to grab his spear – his fingers brushing along the fine grass blades – but then felt the blade pulled out of him, releasing a gushing 'waterfall' of blood from him and causing him to fall to the ground as the pain rushed through the broken roots of his nerves. The bandit above raised his sword again, to slash at his skin once again. The world around Leo had seemed to have slowed down as he watched his body bleeding, dying... Alex's angered cries seemed to echo through Leo's ears as he heard Alex running towards him, whereas Sarah simply stood fearfully, her eyes watering with crystal teardrops. Leo didn't want to leave them, but he had no choice; he would die anyway. Yet still his body refused to let go.

Let me go...

– 0 –

'LEO!' a muffled, crying shout was heard. Leo suddenly realised – he was nowhere near death; it was far worse. Leo's eyes and body shook fearfully as he looked at his hands – hands drenched in thick drips of blood. It covered his hands, catching under his nails, and his robes were covered too. Then he realised with horror what had happened.

Leo looked around him, seeing all of the bandits slumped on

the ground, pale white and dead. Covered in thick, piercing scratches, their eyes with no life left. Leo looked at the dead bodies sorrowfully, then unwilling turned to face Sarah and Alex, both of whom were shocked. Sarah's eyes were filled with tears, whereas Alex stood with complete desperation at what to do. Leo then suddenly knew it.

He lunged down onto the floor trying to get the blood off his sore hands. His hands were burning like a roaring fire – as if they felt the emotion he was suffering. He was almost screaming as he wiped the dark blood into the soil and grass. He even felt his own eyes water, just thinking about what he had done. Eventually, all his energy was gone and he was reduced to thumping down pathetically onto the ground in weakness. He suddenly lurched as he felt the pain from his wound retaliate from his movements.

He felt a hand gently placed on his shoulder and then looked to see Sarah kneeling beside him. One hand was to her trembling lip, whilst the other on his shoulder.

"You're hurt, we've got to cover the wound," she said, and then pulled out some white cloth strips from her bag.

"Wh–' Leo managed to begin through his mouth, still dripping heavily with thick ruby blood. Sarah flinched as he began speaking. She gently smoothed across the deep blade cut. Leo sneered in pain as she brushed along, but then felt the soothing healing that she delivered. The wound stopped bleeding, but remained nevertheless.

"Why did... did you flinch?" asked Leo. Sarah then looked into his mesmeric green eyes, but then looked away without an answer. She wrapped the bandages around carefully as Alex walked over to him.

"What happened?" he asked, sitting beside him resting his hand on one knee. Leo looked up at him and, unusually for him, felt his anger pulse. How was he meant to know what happened? He was unconscious through whatever had happened! Leo gritted his teeth to hold his rage.

"Shouldn't I be asking you that?" he muttered, recoiling as a bandage pin scratched his skin. Alex looked at Sarah for a moment and then stood up. Both he and Sarah helped Leo back onto his legs.

"C'mon," said Alex, "Let's set up camp away from here. Of

all the things on this world, I hate the dead..."

— 0 —

It must have been at least an hour's stumbling walk they took before Alex found a good spot to camp. After the tent's appeared from Eldred's magical feather, Leo simply took his own tent and said no more. What on earth happened? Leo could still smell both the blood and the fear in his hands. But, what was worse was that he had lost control of emotion. He felt he had failed Eldred completely.

What was worse, however, was what replaced the feeling of death. He no longer cared about other things, but instead wished for pure bloodshed. It pounded in his head, over and over, the great feeling he hadn't truly seen or experienced. He could feel his heart beat faster just at the very thought and his adrenaline level rise. He angrily hit himself on the arm, but it did nothing to cure his lust for blood (except bruise himself). He couldn't take this. He needed Eldred's wisdom; he needed his help...

— 0 —

The next morning Leo arose, he had eventually slept despite his fury. The pain had significantly dropped since the day before and Leo was able to walk by himself alone. However, Sarah seemed shocked over this, and insisted on having Alex help him walk.

It would be at least another two days of travel for the three of them — probably longer with Leo's injuries. What was worse was that it was going to be two days of *silence*. Leo wasn't in the mood to speak with them, and they wouldn't dare say a thing in case he jumped out and randomly attacked them. Leo grunted angrily to himself and continued to drag himself along, supported by Alex.

The first day of travel went by, as Leo had predicted, silently. The only noises were the sounds of eating or drinking and the sounds of their footsteps. Alex managed to get some wood and set up a campfire for them to warm up to. For once, Leo was beginning to hate the silence he had once loved. Then again, there was no uncle or aunt nagging at him anymore. No farm, no work, no annoying arguments – all unwelcome memories. Yet, now he loved noise more then ever: the sound of talk, the sound of his friends. Leo sighed and carefully raised his head to look up at the stars above him. He remembered how everyday he used to sit like this, waiting for the stars to give him something brilliant; something great. Leo supposed he had got it, too – magic was a wonderful gift (or sometimes a curse, he added). But *friendship?* Leo smiled to himself: that was the best...

"I'm sorry," said Leo sitting up. "I shouldn't ha – huh?" Leo wasn't talking to anyone. Leo closed his eyes in annoyance.

Okay, so they aren't always there... thought Leo. He noticed the two candles dimly lit in the tents opposite him and then saw the position of the moon – he must have been sat thinking for quite some time. Leo raised his eyes and clambered awkwardly into his own tent. Sleepy time...

– 0 –

Leo yawned as he felt a beam of light shining on him. Sarah had opened the tent doors wide open, and Leo simply turned to his side, mumbling something that sounded like: "sleep... light... off...'

"Fine," Sarah laughed. Leo grinned as the tent doors blew back closed, but then shuddered as the entire tent vanished from above. Leo abruptly leaned up, to see Sarah holding a small feather in her hand.

"You do realise I can make the tent back into a feather from the *outside?*" she smiled. Leo laughed and pulled on his robe-shirt. He stood up and rolled his sleeping-bag quickly, and then, with a wave of his hand, the bag shrunk to the size of a potato. Leo placed it in his pouch, and walked about as he waited. Sarah seemed to stare at him as he did this.

"What is it?" asked Leo, looking at his robes as if to see some blood stain or something.

"Doesn't that hurt?" asked Sarah, pointing at his waist where he had been stabbed. Leo was surprised too – he hadn't felt anything since he woke up.

"I... I haven't felt a thing," he replied.

"Leo, this isn't... isn't... natural..." she said awkwardly.

Leo was almost taken aback at her comment, but simply sighed in agreement.

"Let me see it. . . " she said, walking to him. Leo lifted his robe and looked too. Both Leo and Sarah almost gasped – what had been a huge blade wound had been reduced to just what looked like a simple cut that any child would get from tripping and falling. Sarah brushed her fingers across it, as if not believing that it was like it.

"We need to get to Eldred, and fast," Alex said, appearing from his tent and transforming it back into a feather. Both Leo and Sarah nodded. Leo knew that this was definitely not normal – hell, being a sorcerer isn't normal in this day and age but super-natural healing? Random transformations? If Leo wasn't around his friends, he'd be crying in anger. It seemed the stars had given him more than just a gift but some terrible curse too. Leo sighed to himself – whenever there's good there is always bad. . .

The final day was much quicker; now with Leo being nearly fully healed (it had some advantages, at least). By nightfall, they finally reached the Academy of Alim. None of them could stop grinning – if anyone was going to find an answer of wisdom or counselling, it was Eldred.

Unfortunately, it was approaching midnight, so they each gave a swift "goodnight" to each other and returned to their dorms. Leo, who was never happier to have reached a bed, simply slumped down onto it, arms and legs spread out. Normally, he'd be worried about all this happening to him. . . Yet, there had grown a deep trust in Eldred: if anyone was going to help Leo, it was him. That aching feeling in his gut about what he said died down at the thought, but there was something worse that struck him in the night – nightmares.

At first, he felt the pain in his waist strike violently but then his eyes were open, but blurred. His breathing was deep and angry, and it almost felt like drool was about to drip down from his mouth. Then, a blurred image was approaching, with his hands raised up to strike at him. Leo, without any control, lashed upward onto the person who fell immediately. His nose suddenly filled with the unpleasant smell of slaughtered blood and he watched in horror as he ripped apart the blurred images of screaming people. He tried to stop, but still couldn't. His

83

body simply wouldn't stop... his willpower wasn't enough; he just couldn't control it...

"STOP IT!" Leo shouted out aloud. Awake, he sat up to find sweat dripping down his forehead and over his entire body, his arms shaking violently and his hands tensed and shaped like claws. Leo collapsed back shaking but managed to fall asleep again.

When he woke up, he remembered nothing of his nightmare...

$$- 0 -$$

What Leo didn't know, however, was what had happened with Sarah and Alex. Although both had appeared to go to their dorms, they didn't. Instead, they snuck out together and quickly made their way to Eldred's chambers. What had happened to Leo was too important – even for sleep.

Eldred was, as expected, sat at his desk, scribbling manically on parchment with a feathered quill. He then dropped it into the gold-painted inkpot and looked at the two through his spectacles.

"Good to see things went well, despite there being only two of you," he said, now removing his spectacles and placing them neatly on top of the parchment.

"Something bad happened last night," said Alex.

"Did you not get the information on the Soul Light, as I had requested?"

"Yes, but this is to do with – well, Leo," said Sarah.

"That child has a knack for the unexpected," mumbled Eldred. He then sighed, "What is it this time?"

"Well... we're not sure," she replied. Eldred looked at both of them curiously.

"Teenagers are so vague – grunt this and mumble that..."

"He, I don't know, transformed into something," Sarah quickly jumped in. Eldred now stood up and paced the room, his hand to his chin, brushing it as his head clicked with thoughts.

"Transmutation is not something accomplished by easy means – only the greatest of aged sorcerers have been known to do so," explained Eldred. "Not even I can do that and I have been a student of the Art for nearly 40 years and have not managed such complex spell-craft, so..."

"So how can someone who has been practising for only months be able to do so?" prompted Alex. Eldred nodded.

"So what is it?" asked Sarah.

"Something unnatural – a curse perhaps, I'm not sure myself. I've never heard of such things happening to novice sorcerers; actually, any sorcerer for that matter," answered Eldred. "What happened in his transformation? How did he act?"

"Well, he had been stabbed, and then, he fell to – "

"He was stabbed? When did this happen?" Eldred suddenly said urgently. "You were attacked?"

"Yes," answered Alex. "It seems someone else knows about the Soul Light."

"The plot unfortunately thickens. So these people attacked you?" asked Eldred. Sarah nodded.

"Well, really it was one man – well, it sounded like a man. You couldn't see his face," said Sarah. "But he said about the Soul Light and how... how it 'belonged' to him. Well, I think he said that."

"Really? This person claims to own it?"

"Apparently so," continued Sarah. "But I remember something else, something about him."

"He said that he would suffer without it," interrupted Alex. "Seriously, Sarah, I thought *my* memory was bad..."

"This is most unfortunate and most perplexing," said Eldred, now standing still on the spot, looking at the floor eerily.

"Perplexing?" asked Sarah. Eldred stood for a moment, continuing his eerie stare at the floor. What was most unusual, however, were his eyes, for the pupils had vanished. Eldred quickly shook his head and looked at both Sarah and Alex.

"Perplexing in that I thought only I was told of the Soul Light from Master Alim. Alim died telling me about it – so how could the information leak to other people?"

"Eldred, if I remember correctly, this person also said that no–one should know about it either," explained Alex. "Which would mean..."

"That there was more than one source of information about it," finished Eldred. Alex nodded in agreement. Eldred sat back down again, pondering and brushing his chin again.

"There's something else as well, besides Leo's transformation," said Alex. "He was wounded deeply, enough to kill him, yet not only did he survive the wound healed in two days. And with no scar."

"Ludicrous! There's no way..." gasped Eldred. "Perhaps this curse gave him something else as well..."

"Wait," said Sarah, thinking. "I remember this happening before, when he first arrived. He said he had broken his leg, yet it was normal after he slept here. This can't be the first time this has happened, then."

There was a silence in the room. Eldred was deeply worried. More and more things were becoming visible about Leo – this was crazy.

"If anyone wants me, I'll be in my room," said Alex, who then left the room. Sarah stood up and walked up toward Eldred.

"Here," she said, passing Eldred the book Leo had taken. "Just make sure you work out this silly mystery – I can't live cramped up in here forever."

"Of course," Eldred laughed, forgetting his worries. "Don't worry, you'll find a new home eventually." Eldred smiled with Sarah for the moment and she then went to the door, but quickly turned back.

"What are you going to do about Leo?" she then asked with concern.

"Don't worry, I will talk to him about what happened," answered Eldred.

"But he says he doesn't remember what happened; when he transformed."

"I will *make* him remember..."

– 0 –

Leo felt his unwilling eyes stretch open, flooding sunlight onto his sore eyes. Once again, it was one of those days where he had hoped he just wouldn't wake up. Leo stretched his arms, rose slowly and got changed. He wondered if Eldred would be angry? No, it wasn't Leo's fault; he had had no control over it. It would be more likely that Eldred would be more *intrigued* than angry or worried. Leo sighed with annoyance.

86

"Then again, he is a sorcerer who can lock his emotions away," muttered Leo. He looked out of the window at a clear view of both the gardens and also Eldred's tower. "How can he live like that? I know I would sometimes want to lose my emotions, but to hide them behind a mental portcullis? I could never do that..."

There was a knock on Leo's door and Leo got up and opened the door.

"Hi," said Sarah, who walked in.

"Hi Sarah, you okay?" asked Leo. Sarah nodded simply and sat down on his shabby, unmade bed.

"I was more worried about you," she said.

"Because of what happened?" asked Leo, sitting beside Sarah. She nodded again.

"Well," continued Leo, "I'm worried too. Everything was going great, but now – as a person – I'm changing. I thought being here would be perfect for me, train in sorcery, learn the truth about my life... but now the truth is too much."

"Oh, Leo," said Sarah softly. Leo looked in her eyes and saw the deep comforting feeling she seemed to spread with her pretty hazel eyes.

"Well, now I know the truth, I guess," said Leo regretfully. "I just need to know why."

"Don't worry, Leo, Eldred will find the answers for you – he has for me and Alex. He's never failed yet," encouraged Sarah.

Leo smiled slightly and stood up, with Sarah standing up afterwards. She hugged him gently and wished him luck as Leo made his way up to Eldred's chambers. Leo paused a moment as he stood in front of Eldred's door, took a breath, and then knocked quietly.

"Come in, Leo," said Eldred. Leo walked in and closed the door behind him and took a seat opposite Eldred. Eldred simply continued to examine the few pages of the *Account of the Soul Light, Origin and Purpose*.

"I guess I should tell you about the past few days," said Leo quietly. Eldred shook his head.

"No need to, Alex and Sarah explained the majority – plus news travels fast. The Loremaster's Tower is a very important part of the kingdom; I was most grieved to hear its libraries had been burnt down," explained Eldred. Leo seemed startled.

"Alex and Sarah already told you?" he asked, shocked.

"They thought it was best – they knew you needed your rest, especially after what happened."

"So, do you know what it was?"

"A good question," said Eldred. "This... transformation... is the most unusual thing I've heard in so many years. I must say you had me completely puzzled when Sarah and Alex told me about it."

"That's not promising..." muttered Leo. Eldred smirked.

"Instead I took a look at this book," said Eldred, raising the book up. "I must thank you for this, I know it's not a lot, but, it's darn useful for someone like me whose been searching for *any* information for over 30 years."

"Not a problem," answered Leo, reminded stingingly of the cloaked figure. Leo still wondered what would happen the next time he went looking for the Soul Light – hopefully this figure presumed he was now dead. Otherwise... well, Leo didn't want to think what would happen...

"Have you read this yourself?" asked Eldred, pulling out his spectacles and skimming through the writing again.

"Yeah, I had to make sure it was about the Soul Light, didn't I?" replied Leo. Eldred murmured, as if to agree, but seemed too interested in the book now. Leo rolled his eyes as he waited nearly a minute for Eldred to speak again.

"Well... Lord Dragir has done his work," said Eldred, finally. "There's a lot more information in here than it first appears."

"What do you mean?" asked Leo, who walked around behind Eldred to look at the text with him.

"Well," explained Eldred, "he tells us what it does, see here?" He pointed along the line, which read '*it keeps the evil at bay*'.

"So it's... a barrier?" asked Leo.

"Precisely: a barrier against evil," said Eldred. "Which is why, for us, it shows us more."

"What do you mean, *for us*?" asked Leo, puzzled by Eldred's comment. Eldred closed the book and removed his glasses.

"It means," said Eldred, "that it can help you."

"Wh– *me*?"

"Yes, Leo," smiled Eldred. "You see, a curse can only be placed on someone when the caster truly means to cause that person to suffer – as such, it is an evil act. Therefore, the Soul Light can block off the curse... even cure it."

Leo had to quickly find a seat; he just couldn't believe it. Of all the things that had happened, all the annoyances and jinxes, it was this that he thought Eldred couldn't solve. But he had. Once the Soul Light was found... he wouldn't have to worry anymore about this curse. Leo would have cried if he wasn't so uptight – it was stupid really.

He had only suffered this curse once, yet Leo was glad to know that it would be gone. He wasn't sure why – maybe he could have learnt to control the curse and use it. It was more the fact that, for once, he found he was actually *scared* of himself; fearful that maybe he could hurt the innocent. Or that it was the first time he had ever tasted *true* fear itself.

"Where?" asked Leo quickly. "Where is it?"

"I'm sorry Leo, but I don't know," said Eldred. Leo's head drooped slightly.

"I'm sorry, Leo, but not until I've looked at this text fully and looked for any hidden meanings can we begin searching. Artefacts like these have a tendency to not point out the obvious effects they might have.

"Also, I hear you didn't scar from your wound..." continued Eldred.

"Yeah, it healed... somehow..." muttered Leo. Eldred moved round to Leo and unrolled the bottom of his robe to see.

"Where was it?" he asked, and Leo pointed around his toned stomach. Eldred could hardly believe his eyes – nothing! There was nothing at all, yet even a slight scratch across his own cheek had scarred him so many years ago.

"I will have to look into this," said Eldred.

"Well, what should I do in the mean time, you know, whilst you find out?" asked Leo.

"What all sorcerers must do," smiled Eldred. "Train."

VIII

Rival Retribution

"When is he going to finish..." moaned Leo, twirling his spoon about in his porridge.

"You've said this *every* day, Leo. I'm sure he's nearly done..." said Sarah irritably. They were sat opposite each other, each with a bowl and plate of food as the golden sun rose.

"But... it's been two months already!" argued Leo. "C'mon, you have to agree, he's taking his time."

"Okay, fine," she finished, rolling her eyes. She then looked gloomily at the bowl below her. "Could you finish this for me?"

"Yeah, sure," said Leo, taking the bowl from her. Instead Sarah rested her head on her palms, staring blankly at the table.

"Have you ever thought he might already have the answers?" she asked. "Maybe he just needs to find what we need to do."

"I never thought of it that way..." mumbled Leo, taking a last spoonful of Sarah's leftover porridge. "Anyway, I'm finished now."

"Okay," said Sarah, helping Leo with the bowls and cutlery over to a large sink in the kitchens opposite the dining room. Leo spent a few seconds holding a wet cloth and it then jumped from his hands, enchanted, and washed the bowls for him.

Both Leo and Sarah then left and as they passed through the dining room's doors, Alex entered (no doubt after oversleeping). After Leo passed by, Sarah heard Alex's muttering: 'sitting in a tree... doing what they shouldn't be...'

Sarah glared and Alex quickly stopped, resisting the urge to snigger. Leo had thought he had heard Alex say something – must have been his imagination...

– 0 –

Eldred had used what must have been the umpteenth spell today. Eldred sneered as another of his attempts failed.

"Damn it, Raiden. Where are you?" Eldred leant over the map of the continent of Asgarth that was laid skewed along his cluttered desk. Eldred was becoming increasingly annoyed and he could feel his shoulders tense in agitation. Eldred took a quick and deep inhalation of air, and calmly released it, relaxing his muscles and releasing the burden of stress.

Every year it gets harder to control my anger, thought Eldred. *Thank the gods Leo has finally arrived.*

Eldred knew his magic was draining from him, but for hours he kept trying, regardless of his diminishing strength. He had to keep trying: Raiden was out there somewhere. There was no way he could be dead; he's not even old. And everyone knows a creature would be lucky to sink its teeth into *Raiden.*

The night approached and Eldred's weary body was slowly slouching. The lack of magic in him made him drowsy, and often Eldred found himself needing to sit down before attempting yet another location spell. Eldred was becoming sick of this spell entirely – it had worked every time before but now... maybe now he was becoming too weak...

"Don't give in, use this," a voice sounded in Eldred's chamber. Eldred suddenly felt the slight trickle of magic left within his mind grow. His mind became sprouted with it, his body invigorated by the arcane pulse of this seed. The feeling of this magic was different, somehow, and it dawned on Eldred that it was sourced not from him but another being; the being that had just spoken.

In a small matter of time Eldred's body had become filled to the brim with fresh magical power, and he instead focussed his concentration to the being that had re-invigorated him, rather than on his location spell.

"You return again?" said Eldred, standing up and brushing away the gathering dust on his map.

"Did you really expect me to leave without seeing Leonard?" replied the voice. Eldred smiled at the thought.

"I guess not... and I assume I'm now in your debt, seeing as you revived my magic."

"You assume correctly... so will you let me see him?" the voice demanded. Eldred wondered for a moment and then nodded, and although this voice was not in the room, it seemed to have registered Eldred's nod.

"When will you arrive at my door?" asked Eldred with a sigh.

"I will not be arriving." A manner of confusion struck Eldred at this person's reply.

"Why?" Eldred then asked daringly. There was a pause between Eldred's question and the voice's answer – a hesitation. Eldred could tell he had taken a daring hit at the person, but waited patiently for his reply.

"If I were to go into the open, terrible things would happen. That is why I am not speaking to you face to face – I am many hundreds of miles away from your academy at this very moment. For now, I must stay here."

"Then how will you see Leo?" asked a puzzled Eldred.

"I have my own methods," it replied. "Good luck with your search for Raiden."

"Thank you," said Eldred. He placed his finger upon the map of Asgarth and felt as the new magic in him flooded down his finger, moving it around. It was moving! Eldred sighed happily – before his finger had refused to move, but now this extra magic was guiding him. Soon his finger stopped, positioning itself onto a city.

"I see it worked," the voice spoke again.

"Still here?" laughed Eldred.

"There is one thing I thought you would like to know: he is nearing. Have you felt his presence?"

"Of course," answered Eldred. "I would recognise that presence anywhere."

"As long as you know, I am sure he is planning something against y– "

"I will warn Leonard," Eldred cut in. A feeling of relief could be felt from the voice's presence. The presence drifted slowly away from the room, and after a few minutes vanished entirely. Eldred's finger had not budged from the city on the map. He instead began casting another spell – and after a few seconds, spoke:

"Hello, Raiden." Eldred waited anxiously, hoping that the spell had been to no avail when it had done so well. At last, a voice came through.

"Trust it to be you, Eldred. What's the problem?"

– 0 –

Leo felt his eyes sting as they did every other day as, each morning, the sun shone brightly through his dormitory window.

But it wasn't the sunlight that had awoken him from his weariness. Instead, there was something prodding him on the arm painfully.

"I wish you wouldn't sneak in on me," he said roughly. He heard Sarah's laugh and Leo felt himself smile as well as his heart warm.

"Well, it's not like you sleep naked," said Sarah. Leo turned over to see her knelt by the side of his bed.

"Besides," she continued, "Eldred's ready." Leo nearly leapt straight out of his bed at the two words.

"He's ready?" he exclaimed loudly. Sarah simply giggled at him and nodded.

"Yeah, he wants to meet us all outside, about midday-ish," Sarah finished, standing up. Leo had never heard such good news. As soon as Sarah left, he immediately changed quickly into his robes, the gift from Eldred, which had been used so much it was more like a uniform for Leo. He grabbed his spear firmly, attaching it across his back with a long leather strap, and then collected his gear from both his wardrobe and his dressing table. Dust had collected on many of the items, but Leo just packed it in regardless and then hurried to the dining hall.

Only Alex was in the dining hall, wearing the same robust clothing of their previous venture. He was sat eating some bread, not saying a word or even looking as Leo passed by into the kitchens. A few minutes later, Leo returned with a mixture of fruits, bread and water and sat opposite him.

Finally, Alex finished eating his dry bread and returned his plate to the kitchens. He returned and Leo looked up; it was unlike Alex to stay after he had finished eating. Alex simply gazed at Leo. Leo, now feeling awkward, quickly spoke:

"What is it?" he asked. Alex's eyes seemed to change, as if regaining consciousness, and straightened up.

"Nothing," he muttered. Leo looked at him, unconvinced.

"No, really, what is it?" asked Leo again. Alex then leaned in, his eyes starring into Leo's. He leaned forward, his chin nearly dipping into Leo's plate, as if he were an interrogator.

"Do you... *like* Sarah?" he asked. Leo felt himself blush and the blood pump to his head. He leaned back, rolling his eyes.

"Why?" asked Leo.

"Do you?" Alex interrogated again. Leo had never thought about it really – him and Sarah. She was great, and too darn pretty, but for some reason Leo felt like his heart held him back. Then again, when Leo imagined the two of them at the time, he felt the butterflies flutter in him.

"I... don't know," replied Leo, looking down at his plate and spinning an apricot. Alex leaned back onto his chair, unsatisfied. Leo had lost the urge to eat, so left his plate and hurried out of the dining hall. Alex stared as Leo left, still pondering over what Leo said.

"He *so does*..."

– 0 –

Leo found himself sat in his dorm for the rest of the morning, his mind trying to elucidate what Alex had asked. The only thing that seemed to form in that time was the lucid butterflies. Leo decided to focus on the matter at hand – if Eldred was ready now, that meant they would definitely be looking for the Soul Light. This curse – yet another of Leo's annoyances – could finally be gone too. Perhaps he would eventually be able to train without all these problems. Leo laughed.

"Yeah right, like that'll happen," he muttered. He let himself collapse on the bed, waiting as the painful seconds slowly ticked by in his head.

After what may have been an hour, there was a gentle knock on his door, causing Leo to sit abruptly up.

"Come in," he spoke. The door opened, and Sarah walked in wearing a simple white shirt and a long purple dress, scaling down beyond her heels. Her quiver remained, like always, by her hip and her bow was carried in her left hand.

"Hey," she said, sitting on the edge of Leo's bed. "You okay?"

"I think so..." he answered, confused. "What made you ask?"

"Oh, well Alex just said you had a lot on your mind. He also said you wanted to ask me something?" she said curiously, tilting her head to one side. Leo found himself gritting his teeth as he blushed furiously. It was so typical for Alex to do this kind of thing. Leo could hardly bear to look at Sarah either – that cuteness that seemed to emanate from her face. Leo tried to

94

speak but began stuttering; his lips were trembling too much. His gut felt like exploding and he could even feel his heartbeat thump harder every agonizing second.

"I... I w– was wondering whether, you..."

"Whether I..." ushered Sarah, leaning closer. Leo felt himself grow even more nervous, fearing for the worse.

"Whether... you..." Leo swallowed deeply. "... you were... doing any more training before we go?" Leo felt his head droop secretly. Leo couldn't take it; he was yet again a failure. He couldn't even say a few simple words to her – what was he so afraid of? After a solitary moment, he looked back at Sarah. She stared at him, somewhat confused, but leaned back from him.

"Nah..." she said, standing up and stretching her arms. "I think I've put in enough practise."

"Can never practise too much," replied Leo.

"Well, I think after the number of years I've practised archery, I can have one morning off," she answered, winking. "Anyway, come on, Eldred will be waiting for us." She grabbed his hand with both of hers, lifting him up onto his feet again. Leo grabbed his wand and strapped his spear across his back.

"Right... let's go," said Leo.

– 0 –

Leo and Sarah were delayed in finding Eldred. After a fruitless search of the garden, they eventually found him in the dining hall alongside Alex, who had already met with him earlier. It was peculiar for Eldred to schedule tasks in the dining hall, but when both Sarah and Leo reached the table their mouths nearly dropped open looking at the great assortments of things scattered across the table. Many spread out pieces of parchment, varying from maps to scriptures. Then, Eldred was fiddling about with Sarah's compass, rotating the dial continuously, one way and then the other. He seemed almost oblivious to the two of them entering.

"We're here," said Leo, trying to reassure himself that they weren't figments of his imagination. Both Alex and Eldred looked up suddenly, both caught in surprise.

"Sorry, Leo, please sit down," apologised Eldred, raising his hand out to the two of them. Leo and Sarah sat down opposite each other. Sarah was glancing over the maps, but Leo's and Alex's eyes were locked for a moment of time: Leo's eyes narrowed and a sly smile crossed Alex's face.

"I apologise for the time I have taken, it has not been easy to know the next best move," said Eldred. "The world is but a chess board and the movement of one pawn can mean victory or failure."

"Do you know where it is now?" asked Leo desperately. He had wanted to hear this answer for so long, but he wasn't prepared for what he heard.

"Not yet," replied Eldred. He raised his hand in peace, as if feeling the swelling of anger in Leo.

"So why are we leaving now if you don't know where it is?" Sarah quickly jumped in and placed a hand on one of Leo's legs. Leo could feel the anger flood away from him, as if Sarah's healing touch had purified him. Either that or he was getting light-headed...

"Because if the three of you can do this one task for me, then many more questions shall be answered. Everything that you do will help us to find it — then our dear friend Leo can be free of his curse," said Eldred. Leo felt his cheeks burn red, but then suddenly realised Sarah's hand had moved off his leg. Leo was confused — that meant nothing; all she did was touch his leg to calm him. It meant nothing...

Eldred had still been turning the compass through their conversation, but at last the clicking noises finished as the dial was turned one last time. He closed the top of the oak compass box and passed it to Sarah. He then rotated a map for them, and pointed at a small dot on the map.

"This here is the port; the city of Arashar, about 130 miles (Alex grimaced at the very mention of 'miles') from here. Head to the Swaying Inn, where you shall meet an old friend of mine: Raiden Philli. When you arrive, he shall tell you what you need to do."

"Raiden Philli..." mumbled Leo.

"Recognise the name?" asked Eldred. Leo nodded.

"Yes, he was in a few of the books at the Tower. He was a famous dragon slayer..." explained Leo. Then it dawned both on him, Sarah and Alex what he had just said.

"Whoa, whoa, a dragon slayer? You must be joking!" said

Alex, gasping. Eldred found the expressions on their faces hilarious.

"Don't you remember? *A terrible guardian protects it?* What guardian would be more powerful, more perfect, than a dragon?" said Eldred.

"Well... I suppose..." said Sarah. "But it's a bit, well, ignorant isn't it?"

"Ignorant in what way?" asked Eldred.

"Well, we're not even adults, and you expect us to fight a dragon? I do hope it's just your age that's making you crazy..."

"Very funny, Sarah," smirked Eldred sarcastically. "And, no, I'm not going crazy. Why do you think I've sent you to a famous dragon slayer? You will not be alone in this fight."

"Eldred... didn't you tell me that many dragons were slain? I thought they were a near extinct species now?" asked Leo.

"They nearly are, fortunately Raiden is well known for locating dragons. He has his tricks and traps," answered Eldred. "When you reach Arashar, Raiden will tell you what needs to be done. It's best to dwell on the matter when you're there; you have a lot of travelling ahead of you." Alex grumbled at the word.

Eldred looked at Leo and his blue eyes seemed transfixed. Leo felt a warmth in those eyes, but it was apparent that Eldred had gone into another of his dazed thoughts again.

"Are you okay, Eldred?" asked Leo, waving his hand in front of Eldred's eyes. He blinked.

"Oh, yes, sorry Leo. I wasn't quite here."

Eldred now stood up and so did the three of them. Eldred started collecting up things from the table, building a manageable pile to take back to his office. Eldred looked up at the three of them, one eyebrow raised curiously.

"What exactly are you waiting for: an invitation? Get out of here!"

– 0 –

Six days. That's what Sarah said: six days. In fact, those two words were able to slay both Alex and Leo in one stroke; mentally, of course, not literally.

They were to travel for a predicted six days, heading towards

97

Arashar, along huge grass plains that seemed to span for infinity. Despite all of this, for what the journey would be worth, Leo didn't mind the painful blistering of his feet. No matter how far he needed to travel, no matter how harsh, Leo was going to be rid of this curse and send it back from where it came.

The first day of travel was one of stoic silence, as if the three of them were marching to war. Leo was unsure why this happened, perhaps the very word 'dragon' was still rumbling around in all their heads; Leo knew it definitely was in his head. The mere thought of a dragon sent his legs shaking gelatinously and the tiny hairs on his back prick up. He trusted Eldred enough to know that Raiden wouldn't let them down in a fight, but that only made *four* people. This was more than crazy: this was suicide.

The morning of the second day rose gloriously, shining a ray of light into Leo's tent. Leo stirred, but was unwilling to wake. Despite how he felt about this curse, his feet had disagreed with him the day before. They had turned raw by the afternoon, but this morning the pain had left them.

Leo unravelled himself from his blanket to look at his feet – there were no blisters, nor any redness. These healing powers were simply, well, amazing. Leo sure hoped that these powers weren't part of the curse – he could easily live with some extra magic.

After a few minutes, Leo exited his tent, fully clothed and awake. He tapped the peg of the tent, transforming it back into a feather and placed it into his pocket. Both Sarah and Alex were already awake, tapping their feet impatiently as Leo emerged.

"Sorry..." mumbled Leo.

"Don't worry, we'll just have to catch up the distance," said Sarah, with a smile. Alex grumbled, kicking the ground. Leo rolled his eyes and sighed, following suit as they began walking.

"So how far have we got?" asked Leo.

"Well, we covered about 20 miles, according to the compass. We've still got a long way to go," replied Sarah.

"I do not think it wise to continue in this direction."

Leo raised an eyebrow: "what did you say, Alex?"

"I didn't say anything!" exclaimed Alex. Leo zipped around

to look at Alex, but instead there was another person – a man whose face seemed grotesquely scarred: it was pale and tortured. A thick black cloak was wrapped around him, held in one of his hands, and the man's pupils were red slits, with abnormal veins spreading across the white of his eyes.

There was a sudden shudder in Leo's pouch, and before he could begin speaking, he felt another shudder. Leo quickly whipped his hands into his pouch to feel the wand shaking madly, as if to break free. Leo narrowed his eyes: he knew who this was. The person simply smiled.

"I come from my master, who bids you congratulations on your survival," he spoke; his voice deep but with a faint hiss. "However, he also adds that your ignorance astounds him; he tried to kill you but you shall continue to search for the Soul Light, regardless. Tell me... why is this?"

"Tell us who you are," replied Leo, gripping harder to the wand. He had to be sure: if he was right, then this person would be no real threat.

"I asked you a question first," he hissed, smirking malevolently.

"We *need* the Soul Light," said Alex, stepping slightly forward in front of Leo. At the back, Sarah remained quiet watching (almost fearfully) what was happening.

"You *need* it?" the person laughed. "There are much more important things than your puny needs, boy. There are much greater powers than you three that require serving."

Leo was feeling the wand grow stronger, and his grip tightened as he felt his pouch tear slightly. He didn't have time for this.

"Let me guess, it is your master's needs instead? Am I right, *Shyam*?" asked Leo. The person seemed to step back slightly, eyes wide.

"How do you know that name?" he said fearfully. "This could only mean one thing..."

With a whip of his hand, Shyam pulled out a wand and slashed across with it. Two streaks of light appeared, knocking both Leo and Alex aside to the ground. He then raised his wand in line with Sarah's throat. She was lifted off her feet, as if an invisible cord was wrapped around her neck, and she was pulled towards Shyam. Sarah was unable to speak, but Leo knew she was screaming inside.

"Let her go!" Leo roared, jumping up to his feet. Shyam hissed at him, his wand still holding Sarah up in the air.

"Tell Eldred that I am waiting for him at Mavros Frourio, and if he does not arrive. . ." Shyam looked at Sarah, "I will kill her."

"You can't. . ."

"I will, boy, trust me," he said. "I have waited for my vengeance – I will not lose it so simply." Then, in a swirling vortex of dark wind, Shyam vanished with a hiss. Leo threw his spear at the same time, but it simply went through the darkness and landed opposite. Leo cursed in anger, not because he had missed with his spear, but because of something else. It wasn't only Shyam who had vanished in the shadows – he had taken Sarah.

IX

Last Words

Leo sighed with anguish, walking to his spear. Alex slumped down on the ground, resting his cheek in the palm of his hand.

"How did you know his name?" asked Alex curiously. Leo hauled the spear from the murky ground and strapped it across his back. He then walked back and sat opposite Alex, drawing Shyam's wand from his pocket. At last, it had stopped shaking and remained peacefully still.

"This is Shyam's original wand – when he appeared, I could feel the wand shaking, as if it was trying to escape from me. I just knew it was him – there was something about him too, something..."

"Dark?" asked Alex. Leo nodded.

"It felt like... he was missing a part of his life, his soul. An empty void in his soul in which Shyam had slaughtered and tortured other people to try and end his own pain. Yet failed..." said Leo. "But this isn't important; we have to get to Sarah."

"Should we go back to Eldred? It's Eldred's business, not ours," said Alex. Leo shook his head.

"Now that Sarah's with him, it's just as much our business as anyone else's," replied Leo. "I have an idea..."

Leo reached into his leather bag and pulled out a coarse map, the same map of Asgarth that Eldred would use. He then smoothed it out flat across the ground.

"What are you doing?" asked Alex, leaning forward to watch. Leo then put his finger onto a small black dot, labelled *Academy of Alim*.

"It's a communication spell," explained Leo. "Eldred has shown it to me before, a few months back, but I'm still perfecting it. As long as Eldred is in the academy, I should make contact, unless my spell goes awry."

"Somebody's getting technical..." smirked Alex. Leo smiled, simply.

"Too much time spent around Eldred."

There was a sudden spark from Leo's finger, his eyes were

closed as he concentrated. His finger remained motionless on the map. Then, there was a sudden rush through his body; Leo wasn't completely sure what was happening. Instead, he decided to try and get through to Eldred.

"Eldred?" he said, feeling rather stupid as he spoke as Eldred could not be seen. Then, the surge of magic rushed away and vanished into the map. Leo hoped for the best and, in only a few seconds, the surge of magic rushed back to him. A laugh bellowed for all to hear.

"I'm surprised, Leo, that you managed to cast a spell such as this," said Eldred, his voice appearing from nowhere.

"Sorry, Eldred, but we don't have time for praise. We have a big problem."

"What's happened?" asked Eldred, urgently. His voice had become much more focused.

"It was Shyam, he's back," said Leo. "He wants to meet you at a place, he called it 'Mavros Frourio', I think."

"Mavros Frourio? I thought that place was only a legend," mumbled Eldred.

"What is this place?" Leo asked.

"It is a place in legend, said to be a huge black fortress that towers as tall as the greatest of dragons," explained Eldred. "It is the home of the Black Mages."

"The Black Mages?" asked Leo.

"Yes, they are a group of demimages formed around the times of the Great Revolt (Leo knew this was directed at him). They are the dark practitioners who work for a master – a master who is thought to be a god among men."

"Eldred, before you continue, there is something else," interrupted Leo. He hesitated, knowing Eldred's reaction would not be good, but continued anyway. "When Shyam vanished, he took Sarah with him. He's threatening to kill her."

"HE WHAT?" bellowed Eldred. A fearful anger seemed to have burst forth from him. "Trust that filthy swine! He will regret this!"

"You're going after him?" asked Leo. "What if it's a trap?"

"I will not be going after him – you will."

"Wh– me? But, isn't he your rival?"

"Yes, this gives us two things: one, the element of surprise. He simply thinks you are a demimage, like him. Not only will he be expecting me, he will definitely *not* be expecting a sorcerer."

"And the other?" ushered Alex.

"The second," continued Eldred. "Is a test for you, Leo."

"I'm to fight Shyam?"

"With Alex's help, of course. A sorcerer must be able to fight, Leo. You have trained in sorcery, in combat, in discipline. Put together what you have learnt to duel with Shyam; for your sake, for my sake, and for Sarah."

Courage was swelling in Leo like a bubble. The charismatic words of his master seemed to create spirit within him – his heart pounded and his hands tightened. This would be his true test – a test he could not fail. Failure would mean death, success would mean Sarah.

"Where can we find Mavros Frourio?"

– 0 –

Darkness: it was all she could see. A piercing streak of light appeared, however, as Sarah finally managed to open her stinging eyes. Still, the room around her was dark, all except for a single burning candle held in an iron sconce. It illuminated the small room.

Sarah looked around her – she had been chained by her hands to the wall by two separate manacles, both pinned tightly into the wall. Alongside the candle was a huge portcullis, blocking off the only exit from this bleak dungeon. Every wall and floor was cobbled and damp, with an acrid stench hovering about ominously. The faint sound of dripping water could be heard in the corner and Sarah felt a chill up her spine.

Sarah jumped as the portcullis screeched up the wall – she had only just realised someone had appeared. At the sight of him, however, she grimaced and looked away.

"Show some respect, girl," hissed Shyam, walking up to her. Sarah refused to budge her head, avoiding his dark eyes.

"What do you want with me?" she said. Shyam laughed.

"You are my bait, of course. How else could I bring Eldred from his lair?" answered Shyam. "Of course, if he doesn't come, you will have to suffer the fate." Shyam held out a cold and hideous hand and skimmed it down her neck.

"Though it seems a pity to cut such a pretty face..." he

103

finished. Sarah shook his hand away and instead stared angrily at him, her eyes narrowed.

"You're despicable..." she uttered. Shyam moved back away from her, his eyes wide and evil. He slapped her sharply across the face and then grabbed her fiercely by the cheek with one hand.

"You will regret that," he shouted angrily. He went to hit her again, but paused as hollow footsteps echoed down the passageway. He let her go, making her head hit the wall sharply, her eyes stinging with pain.

For a moment Sarah had hoped Eldred had already arrived, but instead it was another man dressed in thick black robes. A hood covered his eyes, leaving only this man's chin revealed in the candlelight.

"My lord, I am not interrupting, am I?" he spoke, soullessly. Shyam looked at Sarah, and then turned around to face this man.

"No," he hissed. "What is it?"

"He's coming," the man replied, bluntly.

"Already?"

"Yes, we felt the change in our magical barrier as he entered – he should soon be approaching the fortress' gates." The man bowed deeply, and then hurried out of the dungeon. Shyam merely stood for a moment, gazing blankly at the wall. A sly smile crossed his face and the slits of his eyes seemed to light up.

"My trap is set," proclaimed Shyam, walking through the doorway and shutting the portcullis. "Eldred shall die."

– 0 –

A hazy mist had begun to settle across the vast hills and plains ahead of them. The mists had also shrouded the sky in greyness and blocked off the sun, despite it being only midday. Leo could tell that these were not ordinary mists; there was a strange aura presiding over them as they swirled around his feet.

"We must be getting closer," said Leo, staring out into the distance. "The mists, the aura: it's just as Eldred told us."

"Yeah, except for the distinct lack of a towering fortress, Leo," replied Alex. Leo rolled his eyes and instead began walking forward.

"Don't worry, it'll appear soon," answered Leo. He was instead more worried about Shyam, rather than finding the fortress. Eldred had a tendency to be right about many things, but to duel with Shyam was something Leo hoped he would be wrong about. He didn't feel ready for something like this – he could hold his own, but against someone as experienced as Shyam? It seemed somewhat suicidal, rather than a test of his training. Eldred wouldn't send him on something so dangerous, would he?

It struck him then – something Eldred had told him before about Shyam. The wand was their soul... and to lose that wand would be like losing a part of their soul. So, if one half of Shyam's soul was in the wand and he lost it... that would make him half as powerful! Of course! That's why Eldred had sent him!

Of course, Shyam would still be relentlessly strong, but at least there was a chance of success. Still, taking another person's life wasn't a simple matter. Slaying bandits was one thing – a spell-duel against a trained demimage was something else.

It was only after a few minutes of deep thought, before a towering image fell upon the two of them. At last, Mavros Frourio was upon them, and an awesome sight it was. A huge, black stone fortress penetrated high into the sky with many lean, protruding towers. A huge wall surrounded the fortress along the ground and in the centre was a great keep. All of the stained glass windows were grey and lifeless in the distance, and not even a glint of light could be seen from the monstrous construction. The mists simmered not only along the grounds now, but spiralled around the towers like a viper curled around a tree.

Alex had taken a few steps further than Leo, amazed by an unbelievable awe of the huge fortress. As he stumbled forward, Leo noticed something odd – it was as if Alex had stepped through a watery bubble of air. Leo's eyes widened.

"Alex! Get back, now!" he shouted, drawing his spear.

"What? What are y– AHH!" Alex had ducked in time, only to see a wolf leap over him, its drool gliding through the air. The beast swung around, snarling with sharpened teeth and its back hunched, ready to spring at them again. Its eyes were unlike any wolf's Leo had seen before – they were glowing red with anger, and the tiny black pupils of its eyes remained focused on Alex. Grey, wild fur covered its arched back, and the thick, slimy drool continued to drip from its mouth.

But, both Leo and Alex turned around as the sounds of snarling grew louder. More of these wolves had appeared, almost identical to the first, surrounding both of them. Leo smiled as they slowly edged towards them both – this was going to be child's play.

Leo evoked a flame, passing it magically to Alex, who immediately sent great balls of fire upon the wolves. Leo roared to invigorate his spirit and charged forward, slashing at the furious wolves who tried to gnash at his body. In a matter of moments, the wolves were dead – burnt and speared through their hearts. Their bodies then began to degrade away, blown away in a gust of wind and leaving no remains of their bodies.

"Where've they gone?" asked Alex, in annoyance and disbelief. The flame he had been given had now disappeared entirely.

"They weren't real wolves," answered Leo. "They were magical, probably summoned when you entered the magical barrier, so...'

"What barrier?"

"... that means they must have been used as a trap, which could also mean the Black Mages now know we're here."

"Seriously, Leo, what magical barrier are you on about?" snapped Alex. Leo jumped back to his senses. He pointed at the strange, glowing wall in front of him.

"Look, right there? You walked through it." said Leo. Alex looked completely flabbergasted.

"What wall? Seriously there is no magical barrier here!" he exclaimed. Leo rolled his eyes in annoyance.

"You know what, never mind. Let's just get going, especially if the Black Mages know we're here now," said Leo. Leo's senses had been improving – magic was helping him in more ways than one. In fact, how he learned to look at this magic barrier remained oblivious to him. He was more concerned with the next matter.

The fortress, although in sight, still took some time to reach. Its magnificence continued to consume them as they got ever closer, and its colossal size only seemed to grasp them when they reached the black cobble walls.

"Perhaps we should stop staring upward," muttered Leo. The strain on both of their necks was definitely telling.

"But it's just so... big..." mumbled Alex. Leo tapped Alex's head, quite hard, actually, and Alex finally brought his neck down.

"Perhaps you're forgetting about Sarah?" asked Leo urgently.

"Of course not!" shouted Alex, sounding insulted.

"Just checking," said Leo quickly, turning his attention back to the wall. He stood there for a moment, his hand brushing down the smooth cobbles of the wall. Alex could see the clockwork in Leo's head ticking away, formulating a plan.

"We can't risk the main entrance, especially if there are guards," said Leo instructively. Alex listened intentively.

"Well, we can't exactly climb up these walls?" said Alex. Leo peered upwards, his eyes narrowed in curiosity.

"I thought you said not to look upwards?" asked Alex, irritably. Leo looked back at him, one of his eyebrows raised.

"Well, unless you want to climb up this wall..."

"No! No! I'm good!"

Leo smiled and instead changed the subject of their conversation for something much more difficult; much more challenging. Leo felt the magic rouse within him, filling every inch of his body. Leo moved his hands, the palms facing towards the ground.

"Stand next to me," he uttered to Alex, who quickly hopped next to him. The magic rushed forth from Leo's hands, and the very ground below them began to rumble. The earth cracked around them, broke free of its surface, and soon they were both flying upwards. Leo opened his eyes and watched gleefully, as a small platform of earth levitated the two of them slowly higher and higher.

"Woah..." said Alex, looking down to the ground that was slowly vanishing beneath them. Soon the earth below was gone, and all that could be seen in front of them was the perpetual black outer walls of Mavros Frourio. The cold air whipped around them as Leo's spell began to speed up, sending them ever faster upward. Soon enough, they reached the top of the wall, and Leo controlled his spell to levitate over the wall. Then, they slowly flew downwards on the opposite side, zooming down through mists again. They landed with a loud and painful 'thump' on their backsides, just as Leo's spell finally ended a few feet off the ground.

"Well, at least we're inside," said Alex, standing back up. Leo nodded, looking around through the mists. Outlines of the fortress could be seen, yet an entrance into the towers could not. Not that Leo had a clue where he was going; all that mattered was getting Sarah and then getting the hell out of the god-forsaken place.

"C'mon," he muttered vaguely walking towards the silhou-ette of the fortress' base.

"How exactly are we going to know where Sarah is?" ques-tioned Alex. "I mean, it could take us days if we're going to search this huge thing!"

"We will *make* someone tell us where she is," replied Leo, marching faster.

"Someone? Do you not know who these people are?" said Alex, amazed at Leo. "These are not your run-of-the-mill de-mimages – they're the *Black Mages*. They train in the darkest parts of magic, performing rituals, sacrifices and curses. It's even said their master is immortal! You plan to capture people from a place such as this?"

Leo was taken aback by Alex: didn't he understand? This was Sarah; Leo didn't care about what these Black Mage people did, or how strong they were. He was going to get Sarah back and that's the end of that.

Before he could reply angrily at Alex, they had reached the fortress entrance. Luck seemed to be on their side this day as the front door was right in front of them. Two wooden doors, twice their height, towered over them with a wrought-iron handle hanging motionless in the misty winds. Leo walked towards it, expecting it to be locked or enchanted, and grabbed the handle. Nothing happened. He then nervously turned the handle – it wasn't even locked! Luck really was on their side...

"It's not locked," said Leo happily. "Lazy guards?"

"Perhaps," smiled Alex. "Then again their guards were probably those wolves. Can wolves lock doors?"

The door swung open, squeaking as it turned, to reveal a grimy stone room. It was rather small for an entrance and not a single feature was in the room only some candles mounted on rusting sconces. The room itself split into three corridors, each dimly lit by further sconces.

"Which way?" asked Alex puzzled. Leo stroked his chin as he thought.

"We'll take our chances," he replied. He went to walk towards the corridor in front of him, but there was a change in the air. Magic was at work somewhere. Leo jumped back quickly as a solid cobble wall slammed down in front of the wall. He looked to his left to see this corridor blocked off too. The entrance door slammed closed and a loud 'click' could be heard. Alex ran to the door, trying to open it but it*had now been locked. Only one passageway remained.

"Leo, this is a trap," said Alex.

"Yeah... I think it is..." said Leo nervously. He peered down the corridor: only the dim candlelight could be seen. Strangely, the candles seemed to burn stronger and the corridor became shining bright.

"Someone wants us to go down here," muttered Leo. "Guess there's only one thing we can do..."

"That is?"

"Spring the trap," answered Leo. He smiled – he knew he was being ignorant, even reckless. Although it went against what Eldred had told him, he was more concerned about Sarah than any sorcerer conduct code.

With no choice, the two followed down the eastern passageway and as they passed each candle, a flame burnt away leaving the path behind them pitch black. Someone was leading them somewhere – most likely Shyam. There was fear growing in Leo: if this were true, then he would have to face him.

It was in this moment that Leo realised how unlike this was of him, how chaotic his mind was becoming. He was breaking the Way of the Sorcerer. He knew this, yet continued to ignore the fears racing through his mind but regardless he continued. He couldn't be reckless, not unless he wanted to die.

The corridor ended, leaving no time for thought. Instead, a staircase in a cylindrical room led upward – this must be one of the towers. As both Leo and Alex entered the room, the doorway behind them was shut off by yet another magic wall, blocking their pathway again.

"Up we go..." said Leo nervously. Leo stepped forward first, followed shortly by Alex. There was a grim silence between them as they climbed up the staircase. In fact, the staircase seemed to be an epic challenge in itself. It was huge, seeming to continue for an eternity.

"You seem nervous," said Alex, who had obviously become uneasy with the silence.

"Well, yeah. Eldred expects me to take on his rival – I have a lot to contend with," replied Leo.

"Well, don't forget I'm going to be helping. And I'll let you in on a secret too – I'm nervous as well. Probably just as much as you," said Alex honestly. Leo looked at him but said nothing. This was the first time Leo had ever heard Alex say he was nervous; he had always seemed so strong. Alex's look, his posture, it was all a disguise really. He was just as human as they were.

Well, just as Flamedra, Leo corrected himself with a smile.

At long last, the staircase ended. It finished in a spherical room, but the roof, rather than being cobbled, was glass. A black frame surrounded the glass, but the misty sky above could be clearly seen. The oak door in front of them was opened by Leo, revealing a long glass corridor suspended in the air. The floor was a strange material, like a metallic wood, but even so Leo was worried he could fall right through it. They were miles up in the sky with nothing but the ground below in which to crash down upon. The corridor itself stretched far and seemed to link the two tops of the fortress.

"Leo, I need fire," said Alex, his eyes slowly turning a fiery orange.

"Why?" asked Leo, confused. He then looked at Alex's eyes to see where they were looking. At the far end of the corridor, Shyam stood, glaring sinisterly.

Leo magically evoked a flame in his palm. Alex took it instinctively, manifesting the single flame into two large fireballs, each one glowing brightly in each hand. Leo drew his spear slowly, his eyes fixated on Shyam, who was now pacing towards them.

"Where is Eldred?" he bellowed, his tiny figure slowly growing closer towards them. Neither of them answered.

"Don't be so foolish," he shouted. "Answer me or I will kill you!"

Again, neither Alex nor Leo replied. Shyam drew his own

spear – a maple pole with a large, steel blade on its end.

"Last chance," Shyam said, a sly smile passing across his face. Leo knew his and Alex's name were on the end of his spear – or the end of his spell.

"Fine then," said Leo.

"Ohhhh," Shyam hissed, "the runt is going to speak, is he?"

"Yes. . ." mumbled Leo, his head lowered. "Eldred sends a message."

"He does? What does the fool have to say?" asked Shyam. Leo looked up fiercely into Shyam's eyes, his own eyes narrowed and his fists clenched.

"EAT THIS!"

Simultaneously, Alex shot forth one of his fireballs onto Shyam whilst Leo sent a ray of energy from his finger. Shyam hissed in anger, jumping back to avoid the assault and pulled out a wand in his opposite hand.

"Fools! You should never mess with a Black Mage!" he hissed, spinning his wand around him. A funnel of fire was blasted at Shyam, but it seemed an invisible shield had been cast around him, and the flame merely crashed into it.

Leo ran forward, channelling magical energy in his spear. Shyam sent an orb of acid towards Leo, but he rolled to avoid it, continuing his charge. Shyam was ready to brace Leo's attack, but before he could Alex attacked too from a distance with another fiery inferno. Shyam jumped back to avoid it, but left himself open for Leo, who plunged his spear at him. It stopped on Shyam's magical shield, and for a second nothing happened. Then, like the shattering of glass, the shield was destroyed.

Shyam raised his spear up swiftly, Leo doing the same and shifting his stance back. Alex held his fire as he waited for the opportune moment.

"Your magic is weak, Shyam," mocked Leo, smiling almost arrogantly. Shyam hissed angrily. Instead of replying, he jabbed his spear at Leo. Leo deflected it, but was not fast enough to avoid the butt of Shyam's spear cracking against his cheek. Leo almost dropped from the hit, spitting blood.

Leo knew too well what was going to happen – his mind could see it: Shyam's spear plunging down his back. He rolled through Shyam's leg and leapt back onto his feet. As Shyam spun around to strike at Leo, Leo quickly cast a spell (a spell he

111

had been longing to try). Shyam felt his balance fail and fell over onto what seemed like oil on the floor.

"Now!" roared Leo, leaping back away from Shyam and the oil. Alex took aim and fired with fire, aiming not at Shyam but the oil itself. Shyam back-flipped acrobatically, avoiding the oil and the fire's path.

Strangely enough, this oil didn't seem to act naturally. The magical conjuration of it seemed to have made it a tad explosive. A thundering bang and a large, fiery explosion shattered the glass and singed the floor. Fire was scattered everywhere on the floor, burning and turning the corridor into something much more like a battlefield.

Alex drew his shortsword, trying to slash at Shyam in the distraction. Shyam, however, was so enraged with the two of them he span around with his spear. It narrowly missed Alex, but a second slash caught his side, cutting him badly.

"Alex!" Leo yelled. He ran, jumping across the flames and slammed into the side of Shyam with his body. Shyam, caught flat-footed, shouted in pain and smashed into the glass framework, shattering more glass. Blood dripped down Shyam's back, for the glass must have pierced into his back deeply.

Leo called forth what energy he had left, Alex doing the same too, and both sent cones of magical fire at him. Shyam slashed with his wand, trying his best to hold against them with another magical shield. Shyam struggled as he held onto his wand with both hands (dropping his spear), finding himself slowly moving back as their attack overwhelmed him. He gave up on his shield and instead slashed with his wand, sending a spell towards them viciously, but not before being hit by the great fire that raged at him.

Shyam's spell had hit both of them; a green streak of magic had sliced at them, cutting their bodies. But they both knew their spell had hit as well. The spell sent at them had been strong enough to knock them to the floor, but when they looked around to see Shyam, he wasn't there. Leo quickly jumped to his feet, only to see two hands gripping tightly on the side of the platform. Shyam was both hissing angrily and whimpering fearfully. His left hand slipped, dropping his wand and now he stared fearfully at the depths below him.

Leo stared down at him.

"Any last words?" asked Leo, Alex standing to the side of him. Shyam, suddenly stopped hissing and cursing, his eyes widened, staring at Leo's pouch.

"My wand..." Shyam's hand let go and he fell, with no scream or plea to live. Leo looked at his pocket, to see Shyam's wand partly revealed. Leo looked down through the mists, but Shyam could not be seen.

"Have it," said Leo, almost in pity, letting the wand sway down in the wind.

"Let's go, Alex."

X

The Fall of Marvos Frourio

Sarah's eyelids drooped as she waited, unable to do anything. She couldn't stand this, the boredom, the silence. She had already tried to get out of the manacles, but they were securely bolted into the wall behind her. Instead, she was forced to wait, her stomach aching with hunger, her mouth dry with thirst.

Her wrists had become red and sore with pain where she had struggled hard to slip her hands through the manacles. No matter how hard she tried, she could not free herself. Magic, it seemed, braced her hands preventing her escape.

At last, her ears pricked as footsteps could be heard coming towards her. She arched her neck to look down the corridor through the portcullis – three men were coming.

The portcullis was lifted and the three men entered. Two were clothed in dark plate armour, they're eyes dreary and both with swords by their sides. The central figure, Sarah recognised instantly.

"It's you..." she muttered through dry lips, glaring at him with her narrow amber eyes. A small laugh was heard from his hidden face, covered by the black hood. It was him – the one who had threatened them, attacked them with bandits and now stood before Sarah, holding her prisoner.

"Ah, so there is intelligence as well as beauty? I am impressed," he said, as his two guards laughed. Sarah ignored the sarcasm and instead pressed on.

"What do you want with me?" she demanded angrily.

"Me? Well, I don't want you here, it is Shyam who wanted you here. No doubt you realised you were the bait for his rival Eldred?" he replied, his voice returning to its normal (yet dark) tone.

"Yes, but Shyam won't win."

"You are indeed a silly little girl. You think good always defeats evil, like every other ignorant fool in this world. Well, we, the Black Mages, *are* the good of this world. Eventually, we shall show the King and his petty lords how to bring peace to this continent. Only then, will we – the good – defeat the evil of this land."

"How can you say you're good?" asked Sarah, her eyes watering. "You murder people."

"Murder! Murder? she says it like it is a bad thing! Do you think people are innocent? Innocence is a point of view, there is no such thing!" he bellowed. "We are soldiers at war; no–one is innocent."

The figure waved his hand at Sarah, and the two manacles opened magically. Sarah rubbed her wrists as she was released. Her eyes widened though – how could he have done that without a wand? She picked up her leather bag, laid askew in the corner of the room and walked back to them.

"Come," the man commanded. "And don't try to escape."

– 0 –

The end of the glass corridor, high in the sky, had led to a small chamber room. Leo sat beside Alex, who was tending to his wound from Shyam.

"You alright?" asked Leo. Alex nodded.

"I may not heal as fast as you, but this isn't serious," he said, yet even his hand was covered in blood from the wound. Leo helped Alex wrap a bandage around his waist and stood up, wiping his spear clean of the debris it had collected. He pulled out his water–skin and took a quick slurp of much needed water.

"Ready?" asked Alex, who had stood up beside him, yet clutched his side in pain. Leo knew he wasn't alright at all, but he knew Alex would be too stubborn to admit it. He smiled and nodded instead.

"Okay, let's move," he said.

– 0 –

Rather than another staircase to go down, it seemed that they had entered the main block of the fortress, a labyrinth of corridors, doors and portcullises were everywhere. Leo would have truthfully preferred doorways to be blocked off as before, so at least he knew which way to go. Leo rotated around the room, puzzled.

"Any suggestions?" he asked Alex, his arms raised upward. Alex shrugged.

"You're the brains here, you work it out," answered Alex in a just as puzzled tone. Leo now regretted saying they would search the fortress to find her.

"What's that?" whispered Alex. Leo spun around again, this time looking towards the far corridor. His ears tweaked and he could hear footsteps. Someone was coming.

Without thinking, he grabbed Alex and lunged into a random doorway, closing it silently behind them.

"What do you thi..."

"Ssh!" hissed Leo, as he placed his ear to the door. The footsteps stopped, some distance from where they were and a portcullis could be heard screeching upward. Leo felt a jab in his side.

"One sec'," said Leo, pressing his ear harder. He felt another annoying jab and turned around.

"What? What is so damn important?" he yelled, but it had come apparent they had stumbled into a room, a room absolutely filled with bottles: shelf upon shelf of bottled substances. Leo stood up, his mouth gaping open in amazement as he looked around.

"That's a lot of bottles..." mumbled Leo weakly. Alex nodded. Leo then felt a trickle of magic in the air, these weren't just any old bottles. He walked up to one, blowing the murky dust away and reading the small label – *Smoke Draught*

"Alex... these are potions," said Leo excitedly. Alex snatched the bottle quickly, staring at the label.

"Hey, cool!" he said, watching the black smoke swirl inside the bottle. Leo picked up another bottle and read – *Flight*.

"Wow, this is some impressive magic," said Leo, uncorking the potion to smell the bottle.

"BRING THE GIRL IN HERE!" yelled a voice. Leo and Alex spun around – it had to be Sarah. They had brought her up here. Leo quickly corked the potion and took back the one Alex held, and dropped them into his pouch.

"Hey!"

"I have an idea," said Leo determinedly. He placed his ear against the door hurriedly and listened. He heard the slam of a door – then there was nothing but an eerie silence.

Leo turned the brass door handle and opened it carefully. Looking round the corner, he could see two absent-minded guards standing outside the opposite door. Leo turned to Alex silently, placing a finger on his lips. Alex nodded. Leo then tried to show with his fingers that there were guards outside.

Eventually, Alex guessed at what he meant, more through sheer luck than through wit. Alex drew his shortsword, and Leo his spear.

"3... 2... 1... WRAGH!" They both lunged out from the doorway, smashing their door from its hinges and plunging their blades into the guards. The guards simply stood, dumb struck and spluttering blood, then both dropped to the floor dead. They sheathed their weapons quickly, and Leo quickly snatched some spare daggers from the bodies.

"Just in case," he said to Alex, winking. He tucked the four steel daggers along his leather belt and opened the door in front of them.

Yet another cobbled walled corridor stretched in front of them, but this time voices in the distance could be heard. An identical door was at the opposite end, open and unguarded.

"Keep quiet," whispered Leo, crouching and slowly moving towards the door. Alex did the same, but his breathing was still heavy from the pain of his wound. Together, they moved silently over to the door, peering in before entering.

The room was a giant circular room, with marble floors, and instead of the usual plain cobbled walls; these walls were decorated with strange drawings. Runes surrounded the edge of the floor, glowing blue mystically.

A ring of black-cloaked men were in the room, surrounding one singular figure who stood tall and proud, wearing his own black robes. Guards in black-plate armour with sheathed longswords made a further outer circle and kept watch over the area. Leo's eyes were fixed on two of the guards – Sarah was with them.

He nudged Alex and pointed towards Sarah. However, before Alex could say anything, the figure in the room had begun talking.

"As you all may or may not know," he started, "the existence of the Soul Light has become known to other people, to enemies. How this has happened, I do not know – I have read your minds and I know that none of you are traitors. You have all served me well and in return I have given you the key to power. Soon enough we shall know freedom. However, there is one person who must first face justice for his treason against us, his failure to us. Brook."

A man started jittering in fright as the figure turned to him. "Master..."

"Lower your hood," the master commanded. The man Brook lowered his dark hood, revealing his bald head and thuggish face. His lips were trembling and his hands shaking.

"Please master, please..." he pleaded, his eyes watering with horrific fright.

"Hand me your wand."

"No... please..."

"GIVE IT TO ME!"

Brook had no choice, for a fear had surged around the room from every figure inside. Alex and Leo watched nervously, knowing something terrible was about to happen. Brook reached into his black robes and revealed a mahogany wand with a gold handle. He handed it to his master and then lowered his head. The master smiled.

"That wasn't so bad was it?" he laughed evilly. "But you know what you have done – you have failed yet again, Brook. Your futile attempts have become senile, your honour destroyed. How could you not assassinate our enemy?"

"I – I... he – he – he stop – stopped me from – doing any anything – I – I was – was '

But before Brook could finish, the master had snapped Brook's wand in two. Brook clutched his chest and collapsed to the floor on his knees gasping for breath, his eyes wide with shock. Leo knew that the master had snapped not only just Brook's wand, but half of Brook's soul as well.

"You time is up, Brook. I offered you the chance for greater power, to be an awe-inspiring demimage. You could have had everything you wanted, like these men will have one day, but you are a failure, a despicable fool who cannot even do his master's bidding!"

And even before Brook could plead for mercy or run, he let out a blood-chilling scream as his master placed his finger on his forehead. A flash of black magic swirled down his master's finger and Brook fell dead, his eyes empty and his flesh burnt away. The master turned to the rest.

"Mavros Frourio, as great as it is, will soon fall. It is no longer required in our search for the Great Journey, when we shall have freedom. But, as you all know, we need the Soul Light. We must widen our search, you have been taught well in the Art, and now we are ready. We shall seize the hierarchy with one swift stroke!"

A cheer erupted in the room from both demimages and the warriors around that stood in watch.

"But in our knowledge of our enemies, we must hunt them down and assassinate them before they intervene with our Great Journey. The Great Journey shall not be stopped," he shouted, with great charisma. He then waved at the two guards holding Sarah, who brought her forward.

"And here stands an enemy of our Great Journey, one who sabotages our plan for freedom and justice," he announced, grabbing Sarah by the arm tightly. The cloaked demimages around her laughed, some manically and others cackling.

"But she's not alone, oh no," the master continued, "she had friends with her too. Perhaps she would like to tell us where they are?"

"Not until I know your name," said Sarah, rather bravely for her. The others around had fallen silent.

"You ask his name?" squawked a woman's voice from under her hood. "How dare you.'"

"Enough, Lilith. She shall die, regardless, so knowledge can be her friend for her last day," he said strictly. The woman Lilith, who had stepped forward to speak, stood back with an apology. The master turned back to Sarah.

"My name... is Rais. I am the leader of the Black Mages, who stand before you now. And yours?" he added, mockingly, making the demimages laugh in evil glee. Sarah simply stared at him.

"Sarah."

"Well, *Sarah*, if you would accede to my request?" said Rais. Sarah stood dumbstruck – what the hell did 'accede' mean?

"Erm... I..."

"Not as bright as I thought?" he laughed, pacing around her. "I shall make it plainer, Sarah, where are your two friends?"

"I don't know," she implored.

"Lies are sins, girl," said Rais, almost happily. He turned to look at the circle of demimages and warriors around him.

"One of you will have the honour of killing this rebel, a saboteur of the Great Journey," announced Rais.

"No..." whispered Leo in panic. He knew Sarah would have screamed or run, but there was nowhere she could go. Even on her face the terror seemed to have frozen her mouth from speaking.

"I'll do it," said a man, stepping forward and lowering his hood, revealing his face. Short blond hair, spiked and a strange tattoo marking his face.

"Very well, Odin."

The man, Odin, drew his gleaming longsword, emblazoned with rubies and his wand in the other hand.

No, this can't happen, thought Leo, as he watched Odin and Rais. Alex watched, just as terrified. Leo didn't want this to happen, this *wouldn't* happen.

Odin was cleaning his blade ready for the killing strike. Two guards walked over to Sarah. Leo had to take his chances – she was not going to be killed. He took his bag and fumbled through it.

Sarah was pushed forward so her neck was lowered to be cut. Odin finished wiping his blade.

Leo had grabbed the bottle, he nudged Alex and they both leapt up desperately.

Odin raised his blade.

Leo leapt through the door, an inky bottle raised in his right hand, a dagger in the other. The scene seemed to freeze as he jumped in the air, the Black Mages looking toward their intruder in slow-motion. Leo roared and threw the bottle down at the ground.

Black smoke exploded everywhere, covering the entire room. Screams and shouts erupted, and Odin dropped his sword in surprise, choking. Swords were unsheathed, but the smoke blinded the remaining demimages and warriors. The men had let go of Sarah and Leo threw his dagger sharply.

A man screamed in pain – who it was Leo did not know, nor cared, for the smoke had filled the room entirely. Leo wrapped his cloak around his mouth and ran forward, Alex close to his heels. He ran blindly and reached out with his hand, grabbing Sarah's wrist and pulling her along.

"Leo?" she shouted, but Leo dared not to speak until the smoke was gone. A door on the opposite side had burst open; Leo cast his spell quickly to see through the black fog of smoke. Men had burst forth a door to his side, but only to choke and fall to the floor. He burst into a sprint, grasping Sarah and Alex tighter to escape the room.

The sound of rushing winds could be heard, Leo looked behind him as he ran to see the smoke gone and Rais staring down the corridor at them.

"DON'T GO AFTER THEM! JUST GET OUT OF THIS FORTRESS, NOW" he commanded to his Black Mages, who leapt up, some teleporting, others running or magically flying away.

"LEO? WHAT THE HELL ARE YOU THINKING?" shouted Alex as he followed Leo. Leo ignored him but instead spun his bag to his chest to look inside. He hadn't stopped fleeing – instead he was frantically running around, putting as much distance between them and the Black Mages as he could. He whipped out the second potion and drank it, not sparing time for thought. His feet seemed lighter than usual and eventually his body felt as light as air itself.

He hadn't let go of Sarah since he started. He was *not* losing her again. Leo stopped quickly and put his hand onto a wall. The wall exploded away, leaving a gaping hole out to the mists of the air.

"Sarah, grab hold of Alex. Alex, grab hold of me," said Leo. They did so quickly.

"Wait, Leo, what are you – AHH!"

Leo had leapt out of the hole, dragging the two of them with them. Both Alex and Sarah had closed their eyes, waiting for the cataclysmic crash to the ground, but instead they seemed to hang suspended in air. The potion of *Flight* had worked, yet for how long had never been stated. Leo flew swiftly downward, over the outer walls and as far as his muscles could manage. Although his flight was graceful, the muscles of his arms ached as he held on to both Alex and Sarah.

There was the sound of crashing rock, and the three turned to look towards the fortress. Great streaks of purple lightning struck the fortress, destroying towers and ruining its architectural beauty. Lightning continued to rain down onto it, the thunder rumbling loudly in Leo's ears. Eventually, the lightning finished, leaving only smouldering remains of black brickwork together in piles of rubble. Mavros Frourio was gone.

A tiny figure could be seen, glowing purple in the darkening sky through the smouldering mists. For a moment, Leo could have sworn that it could see them, even from such a great distance. Then, this figure disappeared into the sky, leaving a purple streak behind.

During this moment of peace, Leo landed gently onto the hillside, lying down on the ground just to rest. He collapsed, arms and legs spread, breathing rapidly with exhaustion. He had done it – he had defeated Shyam, he had saved Sarah. He had passed Eldred's personal test! Leo placed his hand on his heart; he could feel its rapid beat. His adrenaline was still pumping; he felt he could take on Rais right now. He laughed to himself – yeah right, as if that was going to happen.

Sarah appeared above him, blocking his vision of the sky, and Leo felt his heartbeat increase. Her eyes were watering, but she was smiling more than Leo had ever seen her do.

"Thank you," she said, brushing a finger down the side of his cheek. Leo felt himself blush embarrassingly.

"It's okay," he said simply, smiling too. "We wouldn't leave you behind, ever. This reminds me..."

Leo kneeled up to look at Alex.

"How's the wound?" he asked, looking at Alex's bandage. Alex was still clutching the bandage and his face was drawn in pain.

"Let's see," said Sarah sympathetically, sitting next to Alex. Alex removed the bandage, revealing the large cut he had received from Shyam's spear. There was a lot more blood than Leo had first realised.

"Aww, c'mon, I'll sort it out," said Sarah, taking out the wand from her bag. Leo suddenly felt a twinge of jealousy as Sarah looked after Alex. Leo shook his head.

What the... thought Leo. He shook his head again, trying to get rid of the feeling, but the feeling remained, bouncing inside of him. He shook his head, more violently this time.

"Are you okay, Leo?" asked Sarah, her eyebrow raised suspiciously. Leo felt himself blush again.

"Oh, yeah, sorry..." he mumbled nervously.

"Oh... anyway... how did you get this cut? I don't remember either of you fighting in that chamber," asked Sarah.

"We didn't..." replied Alex roughly.

"We fought Shyam," said Leo.

"Shyam? Eldred's rival?" she said surprisingly. Leo and Alex explained to Sarah what Eldred had told them, how it was Leo's test to fight him, how Leo and Alex killed Shyam, and how Eldred wanted them to find her and save her.

"So... Eldred didn't go because he wanted you to be tested?" she asked, slightly puzzled.

"Yeah, though he sounded like he would have gone himself after he heard Shyam had kidnapped you," said Alex. Sarah blushed.

"We should camp here," she said, trying to avoid the embarrassment on her face. "Give Alex a chance to heal faster."

"Sure, okay," said Leo happily. He need a good nights sleep. Though he still wasn't sure why he had suddenly felt jealous and spent most of his time thinking about it whilst he put up the three tents.

By nightfall, the three tents were up and a campfire had been made from some wooden debris from the fortress (Leo had gone specially to make sure Alex stayed warm). Leo and Sarah sat, warming their hands on the fire, whilst all that could be heard from the now dormant Alex were loud snores.

"Poor guy, he's completely worn out," said Sarah, smiling and looking at his tent. Leo smiled nervously. He rubbed his hands, probably more from his nerves than from being cold.

"It's... so... cold..." said Leo, through chattering teeth. Sarah giggled at him.

"Well, I thought Mr. Sorcerer could do magic? Can't he make himself warmer?" she said mockingly. Leo smiled.

"Made this fire, didn't I?" he said.

"C'mon," said Sarah. "Be a big glowing heater, like the one's they had in the Loremaster's Tower." She shuffled next to him and rested her head on his shoulder, her arms tucked under her armpits as she tried to keep warm.

Leo concentrated on the last bit of magic in him, and in his head he could see the golden sun, glowing rays of brilliant sunshine, warming the lands. His eyes opened and he could feel the heat within him building and soon the heat emitted around him. A faint golden glow could be seen around him.

"Mmm... that's better," she said, huddling closer to Leo. Leo placed his arm around her, gently brushing her soft skin. His heart was hammering, but his mind felt peaceful. Leo couldn't help but smile happily as they both fell asleep together in front of the golden flames of the campfire.

XI

Dragon Slayers

Arashar: the merchant city. It was bigger than expected, spreading far and wide along the sparkling water's edge and the gleaming beaches. The streets were sprawling with shops, taverns and huddled beggars on the street, pleading desperately for a stipend of money.

The city was surrounded by a large brick wall, each with separated guard posts where watch was kept on travellers at all times. Guards patrolled the streets, yet did not enter the murky alleyways – even Leo knew there was something wrong down there.

It had taken the three of them nearly four days to reach Arashar. Alex's wound had been improving well, especially with Sarah's healing magic. However, he seemed content that something was happening between Sarah and Leo after waking up and seeing them huddled together asleep. Leo tried to shrug off the matter, but his cheeks would simply redden and he would eventually be reduced to nervous mumbles.

On entering the city, their eyes were fixated on the wobbling signs that hung from each building's side.

The Swaying Inn... The Swaying Inn... Leo had thought, hoping that somehow through magic or luck it would appear around the corner. Yet, despite their efforts, the inn seemed to not exist. Leo had resorted to asking the guards, yet they seemed just as puzzled as they were.

"The Swaying Inn? Never heard of it, the Oak, however, is well known as a meeting place..." the guard had said, but Leo had ignored the rest of what he was saying. He didn't need to go to *The Oak*. Leo's trust had been shaken with Eldred, but he knew Eldred was nearly always right at the end of the day.

"Can't you use your magic?" asked Sarah, who had sat on a grimy bench to rest her aching feet.

"Well, I just can't imagine how. I mean, it's like a location spell, but I've only ever seen Eldred locate people, never buildings," explained Leo sorrowfully. Leo then lowered his voice, looking about to see if anyone was near.

"Plus, if someone sees me casting magic without a wand, we could get driven out of the city. We can't risk that..."

"Looks like we could end up sleeping with the beggars tonight, at the rate we're going," said Alex depressively, sighing.

"S'cuse me, are yeh new here?" asked a man, strong in build with dark skin and his height towering over the three of them. They each nodded nervously. The man knelt down to their height, his eyes looking around. Who was this?

"I don't mean t'be rude, but I overheard yeh con–ver–sa–tion with one o'the guards. How d'you know 'bout the Swaying Inn?" he asked, his eyes watching suspiciously. Leo simply sat there, slightly confused by his dialect, and just as taken-aback that this man had taken so long to say 'conversation'.

"We – we were asked to meet someone there," said Leo, slightly less intimidated now they were at the same height. The man smiled and put out his hand.

"Name's Günther," he said, and Leo was forced to shake his large hand firmly, followed by Alex and then Sarah, who smiled nervously.

"I can get you t'the inn, but I be needin' to know yeh names," he said, pulling out a piece of parchment from his pocket, looking at it confoundedly.

"Leonard Andale," said Leo, eyeing the parchment suspiciously.

"Sarah Quinton," said Sarah. Alex groaned, rolling his eyes.

"Alexander Flamedra," he said. Both Leo and Sarah looked at him questionably, but Günther simply smiled.

"Yup, yeh be the people I be needin', c'mon then," he said, standing up. The three of them stood up after him and followed him.

"Alex *Flamedra*?" whispered Leo quickly.

"I don't have a last name," whispered Alex. "The only name I was given was Alex; there's no such thing as a surname for Flamedras."

Günther took them down towards the docking areas of the city where hundreds of ships from galleys to fishing boats were being crewed or tied up. Instead of remaining on the main street, however, they entered into one of the darkened alleyways. Leo felt two arms wrap around his own and he looked to see Sarah gripping tightly.

"I'm scared. . ." she whispered fearfully.

"So you're scared of a dark alleyway but not of the Black Mages?" said Leo, laughing. He then heard a pronounced 'ahem' from behind him. Whereas Sarah kept walking, Leo craned his neck around to see Alex looking at them both with his eyebrows raised. He was looking at Sarah's arms around Leo's. Leo quickly turned his head back, flushed with embarrassment.

Günther finally stopped after a few minutes of walking through the alleyways. It was nearly pitch-black by now, even though it couldn't have been later than midday. Günther had stopped and was looking around, pressing the walls and floor.

"It be round 'ere somewhere. . ." he muttered. Eventually, he placed his hand on something and a definite 'click' could be heard to echo. Nothing happened, though.

"Oi! Duncan! Duncan!" he shouted angrily, looking randomly around the alleyway. A head popped out of the wall of a house, dark skinned and with a large grin on his face as the four of them jumped at this sight.

"Howdy," he said happily and waving his long black hair.

"Blast ye', blast ye'. . ." muttered Günther angrily, who obviously didn't like being scared. "C'mon, let us in, they (he pointed at Leo, Alex and Sarah) be the ones Raiden be needin' to see."

"Okay, come in then," he said, his head disappearing back into the wall. Günther stepped through the wall, and, somehow, his body disappeared completely into the wall. Leo looked nervously at Alex and Sarah, who were backing away from the wall slowly.

"Here goes. . ." Leo whispered. Feeling foolish, he put his foot on the wall – but it went straight through! He gave the thumbs up to Sarah and Alex and jumped his whole body into the wall.

Suddenly, he found himself being compressed by magic, as if being forced down a tube, and then he collapsed onto a wooden floor, gasping for breath. He stood up quickly, looking around at the bar-room he had entered. There must have been nearly fifty people in the room, all going-about their business, but they didn't look local. Many were sun-tanned or dark-skinned and many of the people in the room were wearing extravagant clothing or amour.

Günther lifted Leo onto his feet, wiping the dust off him. Soon enough, Alex appeared and then Sarah who were both gasping for breath too.

"Yeh, should o' told you 'bout the portal, can be a bit rough, ye' know," apologised Günther, who guided them across the tavern. A large, rounded barman was cleaning dirty glasses as they passed.

"Three ales, Scott. Oh, an' some wine for t'lady," said Günther loudly. In a few minutes their drinks were ready: Günther threw some coins to the barman and gestured to his three friends to follow him.

Instead of remaining in the main bar area, they instead followed Günther to a separate room where forty eyes snapped towards the door as they entered. Leo couldn't help but feel somewhat intimidated simply by how they looked. Rugged, strong, and even their hairstyles were somewhat frightening. The man who stood out the most, however, was a lone man sat at a large round table.

His head was bald but he had a grey 'doorknocker' beard. A red tattoo went down the side of his face, resembling a dragon and a man fighting. His skin was tanned, and out of all the people there his body was the largest and strongest. He stroked his chin, his mind questioning the people entering before him.

"Are these the people Eldred sent, Günther?" he asked, very well spoken in comparison to Günther who nodded and then took a seat next to Duncan. The rest of the men also sat down, no longer talking but only sipping from their ale.

Almost dumbstruck at what to do, Leo, Alex and Sarah sat down quickly opposite the man who was speaking. There was a hush of silence in the room.

"My name is Raiden Philli," he said, his voice loud and deep. "I believe Eldred has told you what you will be doing, to-night?"

Leo nodded.

"Well, men," announced Raiden, looking around the group, "we have three more to serve our cause against the dragon, Draca. As you well know, I have been looking far and wide for this dragon. Some of you believed he was dead, others of you, continents away."

There was an outbreak of grumbling between people, whereas

Leo sat listening intently, sipping his ale.

"Quiet, please," said Raiden calmly. The group returned to silence. "Our magical detectors have noticed something very large and invisible in the skies recently. It left Draca Isle and returned two days later – this being the home of the ancient dragon Draca, it is very well possible he is still alive today."

"But won't that require crossing the Narlai Sea?" asked one of the warriors, leaning forward onto the table.

"Yes, it does mea...'

Once again an outbreak of chatter had started, this time much more loudly than before.

"Could I at least finish my sentence, you slimy vermin!" shouted Raiden. A few laughed at his comment, including Leo. He found it hard to believe these people were professional dragon slayers. Silence fell on the room again.

"As I was saying," continued Raiden. "We will have to cross the Narlai Sea, but we have an extra advantage on our side. Our new friends here will be able to give us clear passage to the island." Leo felt himself redden in the cheeks as most of the slayers looked towards them. Sarah blushed too, but Alex remained tough and rugged – he never seemed to blush.

"Their magic will free us of the cursed thunderstorms and when we reach the island, we shall commence the search for the dragon. Once found, we shall be best off with Operation 13, seeing as Draca is a very large dragon."

There were murmurs about the so-called 'Operation 13' and some of the men were now checking their gear briskly.

"Draca's treasure hoards will be searched by our three friends first and then we shall split the rest, understood?"

There were grumbles from the men, but they obviously had no idea that Leo was looking for the Soul Light.

"Right, men! Get to the decks and ready the ship for sail!" roared Raiden loudly. There was a scattering of chairs, dropping of ale glasses and then hurried footsteps out of the inn. Leo went to follow, but felt a gloved hand land on his shoulder.

"Just a moment, Leo, just a moment," said Raiden, turning Leo around easily. Sarah and Alex joined them and they each sat down as the last few men left the room.

"You lot okay?" asked Raiden, looking at each of them. They all nodded, somewhat nervously.

"It's okay to be afraid. There's always a spark of fear every time I fight a dragon, but experience helps me survive," said Raiden. "I just called you over to know, well, how good you are in a fight."

Leo couldn't help but smile to himself – if only Raiden had seen what they'd been through so far.

"We can hold our own," said Leo, Alex nodding defiantly with his arms crossed.

"Ah, very good. But, a dragon is a very different creature compared to men and monsters. Not every weapon is going to work, especially if you attack the wrong place," explained Raiden. "Now, what weapons have you got?"

Alex showed his shortsword, but Raiden grumbled.

"Best not to use that," he said. "Eldred tells me you have some very nice magic though, says you're literally 'quite fiery'."

The three of them laughed – that was an understatement, but Eldred would have known that.

"I'm skilled with fire," said Alex, smiling.

"Ah, well dragons are quite resilient to fire, especially seeing as they breathe the damn stuff. But it will be a useful distraction, or even a shield against a dragon's breath."

Sarah showed him her bow.

"Could come in useful," said Raiden. "But make sure you aim for the dragon's underside 'cause most arrows will ping off its scales – or if you're a good shot, aim for the eyes."

Leo was about to draw his spear, but Raiden had jumped in.

"So you're the demimage, right?"

"Yeah," lied Leo – he was glad Eldred had chose his words carefully.

"Well, just blast the thing with what you got," growled Raiden. "Try not to use any magical fire though – won't do a thing. Just do what you can to hinder it and give my warriors some cover. Anyway, let's see your spear, mate."

Leo drew his spear, and Raiden swore loudly.

"How did you get that?" he gasped in shock.

"Eldred gave it to me..." said Leo nervously, looking puzzled. It was just a spear, what was Raiden on about? Raiden must have noticed, because his next question was a striking one.

"You don't know what this is, *do you?*" he asked, his eyebrows raised high. Leo shook his head. Sarah and Alex had shuffled forward to listen.

"This," said Raiden, his hand stroking down the blade, "is a dragon fang."

Leo looked at the blade, his eyes wide in awe. So this was what it was – he remembered seeing it for the first time, thinking it was bone. He had instead decided it were some different way of forging steel. Why did Eldred not tell him that it was a dragon fang?

"This is brilliant..." said Raiden, passing the spear back to Leo. "A dragon fang spear will be very good; it can pierce through dragon scales. Draca is not going to like that..."

"So, when do we leave for Draca Isle?" asked Sarah. Raiden smiled.

"Now, let's go! To the ship!"

$$- 0 -$$

Leo, Sarah and Alex followed Raiden back through the inn's portal and then towards Arashar's docks. A splendid sight met their eyes as they crossed the panels of woods to the ocean's edge; hundreds of ships, some mighty, some small, spread across the docks roped onto wooden poles.

They rounded a corner as they followed Raiden, who walked towards the eastern docks. He then made his way to a brilliant ship that floated taller than any other. Blazing white sails hung from foremast, mainmast and bowsprit. The ship gleamed with polished wood, with glass windows here and there. Then, decorated elaborately in gold on the stern of the ship, there was the name *Thunder*.

They clambered aboard across the gang plank up onto the main deck, where the slayers scrubbed the mucky deck, tightened coarse rope and took up positions – some to the fore top, others to the quarter deck and some down below deck.

"Günther! Ivor! Up anchor!" commanded Raiden, walking about the main deck. Günther and Ivor (a man with brown hair in a ponytail and a handsome face) grabbed a long chain down the front of the deck and pulled the heavy anchor from its sandy grave. Soon enough, the iron anchor was raised and hooked into place.

Raiden had leapt onto the quarter deck and gripped the

131

ship's wheel, then he slowly steered the ship around from the moorings.

"To Draca Isle!" he cried forth, his shipmates along with him, punching the air. Leo smiled as suddenly the fame of these dragon slayers became apparent: they worked together. They didn't stop working either, wherever Leo seemed to move the men around him were busy doing something – *anything*.

"Charles, take the wheel," Leo heard Raiden say, as he let go of the wheel and another man grabbed the wheel. Sarah edged over to Leo.

"Do you know what Raiden was on about, when he said about us giving clear passage across the sea?" she asked (she had no need to whisper with the hectic noises on board).

"I'm not sure, but he did say something about thunderstorms..." replied Leo, going into deep thought.

"But what are the chances of a thunderstorm? I mean, we are out at sea but how can Raiden *know* that there's going to be a storm?" she asked intently.

"Good to see you've been thinking," said a rough voice from behind them. They turned to see Raiden, stroking his chin. "Come with me, I'll show you the journey."

They began following him up onto the quarter deck, when Leo realised something.

"Where's Alex?" he asked, looking about the ship's deck. Raiden pointed to the side, where Alex's head was hung over the edge and his face was rather pale and greener than usual. He then shuddered and Leo had to avoid looking.

"Eww..." grimaced Sarah, turning away with her eyes shut.

"Ah, well, either your stomach loves sailing or hates it," said Raiden. "His obviously does not." Raiden then walked off, followed quickly by Sarah and Leo, who couldn't stand to watch Alex vomit unpleasantly anymore.

They were both taken to the chart house of the ship, a small wooden room that contained one table sprawled with intriguing maps and complex charts. A few lanterns lit the room, as the room was much darker than the daylight outside. Other than Raiden, there was one other person inside – a man of good build, but with scruffy black hair that had been grown down to his shoulders. A large scar crossed the side of his face on both his forehead and cheek.

"Leo, Sarah, this is Kemp – he's the first mate on my ship," said Raiden, whilst Kemp nodded in acceptance.

"But, on to the answers you have been wanting," continued Raiden, walking around to the table and searching through the worn maps. He then reached for one and showed it to Leo and Sarah. On the map in calligraphy were the words *Arashar* and then *Draca Isle*. The island and the Southern Asgarth continent were also shown, respectively, but Raiden pointed at the ocean between the continent and the island. Leo read aloud.

"The Narlai Sea? What's that?" asked Leo interestingly. Both Raiden and Kemp raised their eyes, almost in gasping disbelief.

"Do you not know?" asked Kemp, with confirmed disbelief. Leo and Sarah both shook their heads.

"*The Narlai Sea* is an ocean of constant storm and treachery. It's been enchanted in ancient times to protect the island, most likely by Draca himself. The ships that first tried were destroyed in no time, leaving the last few ships to stay back and warn the demimages what had happened. But not even the demimages could break the enchantments on the ocean. Ever since, it has been a cursed island, rumoured to have riches and, naturally, Draca."

"So, what has Leo got to do? Break the enchantment?" asked Sarah. Both Kemp and Raiden laughed, almost in mockery at Leo, and Leo had to control himself from swiping out and hitting them both.

"Someone as young as Leo," said Raiden (Leo almost growled), "could not break an enchantment when a lifetime of demimages have not been able to. But, Eldred says you are naturally talented, compared to most demimages, and says that you could hold off the storm."

"I can try," said Leo, who looked out worryingly at the ocean through a narrow glass-pane. Sarah placed a reassuring hand on his arm, and Leo felt his spirit fly higher than usual.

"Good, good," said Raiden happily. "It could still be a while before we reach the Narlai Sea, so just enjoy the journey for now."

"Okay," said Leo, but was reminded pitifully of Alex – he wasn't going to enjoy days and days of continuous vomiting.

– 0 –

133

The journey itself was not one of much entertainment. In fact, the original excitement of a sea voyage had been reduced to boredom. Some of the dragon slayers had talked to him, but most of the time Leo spent his time on the side of the ship, gazing aimlessly out to sea.

Occasionally, his mind would wonder how he was going to hold off an enchanted storm. A shielding spell, perhaps, but it needed to be large enough to cover the entire ship. Perhaps his imagination could find a way of solving the problem when the time was right. For now, however, he had to keep his mind calm.

He also made a special effort to see Alex everyday, as he wasn't in his prime. Most of what he had eaten was quickly returned to the ocean in a matter of minutes.

Sarah, unusually, hadn't been seen much by Leo since their meeting at the chart room. Leo was displeased, truthfully, but did his best not to show it around anyone else. He had been sleeping in his own cabin too, so rarely got the chance to see her even before he slept.

On the sixth day, it had become apparent that the usual rustling of footsteps in the morning was different from that of any other days. He quickly composed himself and hurried from the cabin and up onto the main deck, where nearly all the dragon slayers were crowded to the eastern side of the ship. Leo jumped onto the rope ladders to look above the crowd and could see in the distance, perhaps a mile or two away, land ahead. A small island – looking vaguely as if it were a wild bush of fern. Raiden gave a cheer, and the dragon slayers all cried along as well and hurried to their positions.

"Leo!" Raiden cried, as he grasped firmly onto the ship's wheel on the quarterdeck. "Go fo'ward to the beakhead of the ship and get ready to cast whatever spell it is that needs to be used. We're depending on you."

Leo nodded and ran down to the far end of the deck and jumped over the railings onto the beakhead. It was a gold statue of a large cloud with thunder rippling down below – obviously a symbol of the ship's name.

The ship turned sharply as Raiden steered the ship towards the island. The sails were unfurled and soon the ship was making its way quickly forward. The waves were growing higher now – perhaps the enchantment was starting, for the waves were larger and rougher than those of other days. The winds howled in Leo's ears and splatters of salty water splashed onto him.

As Leo turned to be ready for Raiden's word, he saw Sarah appear onto the deck and she was laughing. As she appeared she turned to look down the deck's hull ladder and another man appeared: Ivor. The twinge of jealousy Leo had once felt before with Alex seemed to swell into a painful lump in him. His eyes narrowed angrily, as if he had been betrayed, and he could feel the nerve on his neck pump harder.

"Leo! Cast the spell!" Raiden roared down the deck to him. But Leo had realised the anger that had surged in him was becoming stronger – he wasn't going to be able to cast the spell.

Panic rushed him – his emotions were steaming and not leaving. He spun his head to look at the waves, watching as they seemed to become miniature tsunamis below the ship. It was then, in his moment of panic, when his mind realised the death he would cause, a voice sounded in his mind...

Fuel your anger...
No, I can't, it's not the Way...
These people need you – use your emotion to save them.
No, I can't...
Use it...
No...
USE IT!

"NO!" Leo roared like a lion, his voice echoing across the sea, almost for an infinite moment. His eyes had been closed as the voice sounded in his mind, and he had opened his mind to see that they had reached shore. His hands were clenched tensely and the nails of his fingers were digging into his skin.

Panic raged in him again – his limps trembled. He had done what he was told to resist – he had tried so hard to stop himself. His emotion had taken over; his magic had been corrupted by the evil of his thoughts. Yet one thing stuck out in his mind, more than anything else.

He had enjoyed it.

XII

The Soul Light

Leo looked at his shaking hands, fearfully wondering what evil had overcome his weak mind. How he believed that he could be a mighty sorcerer was dissipating before his eyes – shrouded in storm clouds of anger, fear and recklessness. He had failed Eldred.

Leo felt a gentle touch on his robed shoulder and he turned to see a distraught Sarah gazing into his eyes.

"Are you okay?" she asked with a worried expression, but Leo did not reply – anger clouded his conscience.

"Well done, that spell made these treacherous seas a breeze," congratulated Raiden, swiftly running to Leo. The rest of the dragon slayers had lowered the *Thunder's* sails, dropped the anchor and were now making their way onto the island. He also saw a thoroughly pleased Alex, sat on the island moss, glad to be off the swaying ship.

"Leo?" he heard Sarah say, almost weakly. He continued to ignore her and followed Raiden off the ship.

– 0 –

It was an interesting scene as Leo stepped ashore. Slayers were readying gear, emptying crates of rope and sharpening 3–point hooks.

"Report in," shouted Raiden, as his first mate Kemp came jogging towards him.

"The hooks and rope are being prepared now," said Kemp. "I've sent Ryder and Einar ahead to scout the area for Draca's location."

Raiden's face had changed to become full of deep worry. He looked down at the swamp ground, pressing his leather boots into the ground. It squelched and bubbled disgustingly with slimy-green water.

"Hurry the men with the rope; Draca's under the swamp," said Raiden urgently, his eyes gazing despairingly into the distance where the scouts had gone ahead.

Leo felt a firm hand on his shoulder – Alex had come to his side.

"Well, after this, no more curse," said Alex, apprehensively. "Worth fighting a dragon for, isn't it?"

Leo smiled happily – he had completely forgotten about his curse and the Soul Light.

"Yeah – and you won't have to worry about travelling; by ship especially."

"Ugh, don't remind me," said Alex, his face turning a pale tinge of green, even though they were on the land. Leo couldn't help but laugh, but was interrupted by Raiden.

"You guys ready?" he said roughly. Both Alex and Leo nodded simultaneously, and they stood up.

"Remember, stick to what I told you to do, back in the Swaying Inn," he reminded them, looking about. Leo wondered for a moment, finding difficulty in remembering their conversation, nearly a week ago.

"Where's Sarah?" asked Alex, looking about.

"She was with Ivor, if I remember rightly," said Raiden, now watching the other slayers finish tying the ropes to the hooks. Alex had immediately looked at Leo, who had tried to avoid his eye contact, knowing what would be Alex's first reaction.

"Right, let's move," said Raiden, jogging over with them to the main huddle of dragon slayers. "Men! Move out!"

– 0 –

Operation 13, as it had been called, was still something of a mystery. All Leo knew was that he had to stick with Raiden and do as he was told.

Raiden raised his hand, and the group dropped to their knees and waited for Raiden's next command. Leo, who was beside Raiden, knew why they had stopped. Up ahead, were the two scouts that had been sent ahead. They were looking everywhere in the ferns, and dipping their hands into the swamp.

Raiden stood up.

"Ryder! Einar! Get here, now!" he shouted loudly, the two men looking at him.

"What? We haven't found Draca yet?" one replied, both starting to walk towards Raiden who was some distance away.

"Draca's under the s..."

But before Raiden could finish, before anyone could do anything, a huge scaled claw burst forth under Ryder and Einar, tearing their bodies into the air. They shouted in pain their bodies flying up high into the air. The claw then soon became an entire body, head, wings and tail as the colossal dragon reared up onto the surface. Leo gazed in awe at the creature – for it was beautiful, yet its calmness in action made it terrifying.

Draca's body was too big for comparison, perhaps it were some ten times his height, for it was a towering image. His body was made up of strong black and green scales, each as big as a tower shield, whilst his hide was a pale yellow. Horns followed down his back along his spine and up to his neck. Its black-pearl eyes were huge and glaring down onto the intruders before him. Two horns protruded from the side of his head, and as Draca roared two fiery glands could easily be seen as well as a serpent-like tongue and large fanged teeth. Its wings were like leather, and when spread wide they almost blocked out the golden sunlight. His tail was long and whip-like, with small horns along its top. A large spike was at the end of his tail, slashing in the air wildly.

"Get into your positions! NOW!" Raiden yelled, the slayers scattering around in groups. Raiden seemed distraught at the loss of Einar and Ryder, but at least it had brought out Draca from under the swamp. Draca roared angrily and opened its mouth wide, its glands shooting fire down onto Raiden's group. Almost by instinct, Leo and Alex leapt forward to protect the group magically, holding off the fire.

Two groups of slayers had come to the side of Draca, unbeknownst to him, and were readying the hook and rope. Operation 13 was beginning to make sense to Leo, now.

A volley of arrows was sent over Raiden's group from five people (including Sarah) at Draca. Draca roared with rage again and slashed at the arrows, cutting them down in mid-flight. It then stamped the ground and slashed around at the brave men who attempted to attack with spears.

Leo drew his spear, still standing beside Raiden, but Raiden placed a hand on his shoulder.

"Wait for the opportunity," said Raiden. "Those spearmen are only a distraction."

Leo watched as Draca paid attention to the spearmen,

shooting flame at them and snapping at them ferociously. Leo watched the two groups of men, each man raising their hook and rope.

"Fire!" Raiden cried, and another volley of arrows was launched over. Alex, too, had joined in and shot hot flame at the dragon.

It was for a moment that the black eyes of Draca seemed to gaze at Leo, perhaps with anger or even sympathy – Leo stood confused, still waiting for his opportunity. Then – the moment came.

The two groups at the side lunged their hooks at the dragon and Leo watched as they flew through the air, ready to pierce Draca's skin and bring him to the ground. Then, there was a rumble of magic from Draca – something of incredible power and the hooks had frozen in mid air. Leo looked around – everyone and everything was frozen, yet he was not. He still had his spear drawn as he watched Draca, the caster of this spell; sit down with a somewhat draconic sigh.

Leo felt another strange feel of magic – perhaps his frozen allies would come back into time, but they did not. Instead, a voice sounded in his head.

"What is your name?" he heard, and he soon realised Draca was looking at him directly. He was telepathic.

"Leo," answered Leo, nervously.

"And, where did you get that spear?" asked Draca, his tone of voice much calmer and less threatening. Leo found the question slightly random, but continued to answer.

"It was a gift," he said, looking at it.

"So, you have slain another dragon for just its fang?"

"I knew it was a dragon fang," said Leo hastily. "But I never knew until a week ago: I've never fought a dragon before."

"It seems even a dragon can be fooled," uttered Draca, looking at the different dragon slayers on the ground.

"What do you mean?"

"I'm sure you knew that the seas around here are enchanted?" asked Draca. Leo nodded.

"The fang," continued Draca, "connected to that spear is from a dragon friend of mine; I thought he was coming with important news, so I lowered the storm for him. I would never have guessed that it was an army of slayers."

Leo's heart filled with relief – he had not allowed his emotions to control his magic after all. He had not cast a spell to lower the storm. And he hadn't failed Eldred. It was like a flood of happiness; he wasn't a failure. Not yet, he was still strong – he could still be mighty. Then, he realised he hadn't said anything for a moment, and quickly spoke.

"I – I'm sorry..." mumbled Leo, realising why Draca had asked him about his spear. He sheathed the spear from view and walked closer to Draca.

"I am old, I suppose. So... tell me, why are you here?"

"I'm looking for something, something you have," said Leo.

"Oh, so you came to rob me too?" said Draca. Leo found himself to become increasingly nervous, now.

"Y–Yes, I'm looking for the Soul Light," said Leo. Draca looked at Leo profoundly and almost with shock.

"You know about that?" asked Draca intently. Leo nodded.

"Yes, but apparently I shouldn't, according to the Black Mages."

"I'm surprised, I thought the Soul Light was protected through secrecy – I would never have thought it would be revealed," explained Draca.

"So, how do you know about it?" asked Leo daringly. Draca looked around the men, and then blinked. Alex and Sarah returned to normal from their frozen state. They looked around, as confused as Leo had been, and then saw both Leo and Draca standing opposite each other.

"Leo? What is going on?" said Alex loudly, jumping back slightly as Draca looked at him.

"Seeing as your two friends are accompanying you, I suppose they wish to know about it as well?" asked Draca to Leo. Leo nodded.

"If they keep quiet," said Leo. He glared at Draca.

"Very well, sit. I will explain," said Draca bluntly, the three of them sitting down to listen carefully.

"Over 2000 years ago – yes, I am very old – I was hired to guard the Soul Light. I was told to protect the Soul Light with my life against anyone who dared search for it. Of course, being young and foolish, I accepted their offer. I was being offered a considerable sum of gold and a dragon's wealth is measured by their hoard. I was not going to pass on this opportunity, though I did not know how long I would be in service of the Soul Light.

"Eventually, my retirement came and a new guardian was hired to protect the Soul Light. Not only that, but it was taken to a new location – the Chernos Mountains. I believe it remains there now, though many things change over time – I have learnt that much."

Leo took in as much as he could, and so did Sarah. Alex, however, remained confounded by the frozen slayers around him, and he looked like he could burst into a fit of giggles.

"Why are you telling us this? I would have thought you would have been sworn to secrecy?" asked Leo interestingly. Draca's eyes closed for a moment, as if he were reading his own mind. Then, he opened his black-pearls again.

"You are seeking a cure – something perhaps the Soul Light can give you," he said, watching them carefully. "I think it a good enough reason."

Draca spread his wings wide, stretching them out widely.

"In fact, I can take you there," said Draca. Leo's eyes widened.

"You would take us there?" exclaimed Leo, looking at both Alex and Sarah.

"Well, it's that or be attacked by these dragon slayers – besides, my spell is running out of time."

Draca lay down on the ground, his wings acting like a staircase to his back.

"Get on," said Draca. The three clambered up his wings (with great difficulty) and grabbed hold of Draca as he stood up on all-fours. With a burst of energy his great wings, they flapped hard and they were in the air rising higher and higher. The winds swept hard across Leo's face as they rose through the clouds into the clear sky above.

A magnificent sight was before them – there were pearly white clouds below them, swirling slowly around. Then, the sunlight unblocked by wing and cloud shone upon them like a golden beacon.

"Hold on tight," said Draca calmly. "I'm quite fast."

– 0 –

'So, it's in a different place now?" asked Eldred with deep interest. Leo had cast a communication spell to Eldred, to

141

update him on what was going on. From Mavros Frourio to the skies they were now travelling.

"Yes, Draca's taking us there now," replied Leo loudly, the winds howling strongly in his ears.

"Ah, Raiden won't be happy. However, I have other news for you as well," said Eldred. Leo listened carefully.

"There was an assassination attempt on my life, some days after you left the Academy."

"There was?" exclaimed Sarah. "By whom?"

"A Black Mage – I managed to halt him, however, both of us unscathed. A simple charm on the man's weak mind, yet I believe they will attempt to kill me again.

"Listen to me – the Black Mages have realised my link to you, they know that I am critical to your journey. Rais will not stop until he has the Soul Light – we cannot allow this to happen."

"What should we do?" asked Leo.

"We cannot commune with each other, for now. Instead, we shall cut each of us off until the time is right. When you get the Soul Light, come looking for me. I can guarantee that fate shall reunite us," explained Eldred deeply. "Remember, the most important thing is the Soul Light. Do not come back until you find it."

"Yes, master," replied Leo dutifully.

"Good luck, my friends," he finished and then the spell was cut off. Leo sighed and watched the winds go by, wondering where Eldred might be. If there were assassins after Eldred, could they be after Leo as well? Leo thought it best not to dwell on such thoughts and instead focused on the task ahead of him.

A new guardian – perhaps more powerful than Draca – was guarding the Soul Light now. Leo wasn't entirely sure how he was going to handle this situation, perhaps it was the adrenaline beginning to pump around him. At last, a cure for his curse could be found. Then, he could continue his training in peace, without fear of hurting his friends. He had thought this before, but somehow, he knew he was getting ever closer. He was on the back of a dragon – how could he *not* be getting closer?

– 0 –

In what must have been only about two hours later, Draca was now dropping through the clouds, the air whooshing past them and soon a great spread of mountains could be seen that spread for miles. Then, Draca landed heavily, his breathing still light, and lowered his wing to allow the three of them to drop off. His claw pointed to a doorway on the mountain, made of great iron and stone, leading into a brightly lit tunnel.

"That is the entrance – though I have never entered," said Draca telepathically, lowering his claw to the ground. "I guess this is where I leave you."

"Thank you, Draca," said Leo, starring up at him. Sarah and Alex also thanked him, and Draca looked down at them.

"Good luck, I suppose." Draca turned around, but was hesitant before stretching his wings. Then, after a swift moment, he flapped his wings, sending the grit of the mountain flying around below, and took off up into the clouds. The strong flapping of his wings continued to blow a strong wind below, but eventually faded away into obscurity.

"Ready?" asked Leo, to Sarah and Alex. They both nodded, knowing how important this was to Leo. He smiled slightly and made his way up the jagged mountain path, leading to the great door of the dungeon.

The doorway was of iron and stone, with strange markings carved into them in of some ancient runic language. It stood some ten feet tall and led down a gloomily lit passageway of rock. Leo looked at Alex and Sarah doubtfully, but perservered on down the rock passageway. The small passageway opened to a huge room, one with a thin stone bridge that crossed across to another passageway. Only the pitch black filled the room below the bridge.

As they continued, Leo had noticed Sarah did not seem herself. She seemed shyer than usual and also a few steps behind him and Alex, but Leo did not understand why. When he whispered to Alex about her, he had no idea why either. She wasn't normally shy – she was happy and lively. Leo was actually finding it hard to stay calm, and not because of the dungeon.

"Sarah, are you alright?" asked Leo, giving in to his curiosity. She looked up at him nervously, her hands held together.

"I'm cold," she stuttered. Her lips trembling from the freezing-cold air of the mountain. Leo looked at her sympathetically, and unhooked his robe cloak and threw it to her.

"Here," he said. She caught it, and shyly smiled at the ground.

"Thanks. . ." she mumbled, blushing. Leo became even more confused as her face turned pink – he had absolutely no idea what was going on with Sarah today. Women were confusing. . .

The stone corridors continued, lit by wooden torches that burned magically, illuminating the passage. The corridors continued to twist and turn, some into rooms containing nothing, others into glorious chambers. No matter where they went, the dungeon continued further and further, moving deeper into the mountain.

"Wait," said Alex quietly, stopping and holding his hand out.

"What is it?" asked Leo, looking around.

"Listen. . ."

And as Alex said this, the sound of footsteps behind them could be heard, yet none of them moved. Leo unsheathed his spear slowly and silently, as did Sarah with her bow. She notched an arrow and pulled the string back.

The footsteps halted.

Leo's breathing became hard as he tried not to make any sound, but he gestured towards the next doorway, showing Alex. Alex nodded briefly and walked normally to the doorway. Leo and Sarah came through after and both turned.

Sarah unleashed her arrow whilst Leo sent his spell through the door, catching a Black Mage unaware as he fell to the ground dead. Yet as one Black Mage fell, a swarm of 20 others rampaged through the doorway; spells ablazing.

"Get them!" roared a Black Mage, running after them. The deminage swung his sword at Leo, but was quickly disarmed and slain. Leo jabbed with his dragon spear, keeping the Black Mages at bay. Alex wrapped his conjured fire around his short-sword, and moved beside Leo as they fought together. Sarah, meanwhile, used her bow like a sniper, helping her two friends resist the Back Mages.

They were being pushed back ferociously, for the Black Mages seemed tireless and continued to propel their attacks ferociously. They were forced through another doorway, a much larger and decorated one, as they attempted to parry the attacks.

Sarah's attacks had halted and as Leo took the moment to

turn around to see why, the reason become clear. They were in a room, more colossal than even Draca, made of carved yellow rock, almost like a cathedral. There were stain-glass windows with illustrations of fighting warriors, despite the windows not revealing the outside (for they must have been in the centre of the mountain). Yet, the most glorious visage of all was that of a small podium in the far centre of the room, on top of which stood a glowing pearl – exotically beautiful and surging with unmeasured magic. Even the Black Mages had stopped transfixed at it, wondering what the object was or perhaps realising what it was. For Leo truly knew what it was – the Soul Light.

Leo ran forward, ignoring the Black Mages and even Sarah and Alex. He stood in front of the podium, tall and mighty, wondering what might happen when he touched The Soul Light. Perhaps he would feel the same magnificence as Sarah's healing magic as the curse was thrown out of him, or even a new sensation greater than that he had ever felt. He stretched out his hand, his lip trembling excitedly, and grasped the pearl. He then lifted it from the podium – nothing happened to him but everyone in the room fell silent.

RUMBLE... dust from the cavern fell from its towering ceiling onto those below. Leo looked fearfully at the cavern wall that was before him. Another RUMBLE... Sarah and Alex both stood still, ignoring their enemy and witnessed the sound and shaking of the grand cavern. RUMBLE... The Black Mages stopped gazing at the jewel to watch the ceiling as the cavern shook, each rumble growing in intensity. Then something terrible happened.

CRACK.

Leo didn't wait: he pushed himself away from the wall and ran as hard and as fast as he could. In turn, Sarah and Alex then followed, desperately running after him. Even the Black Mages seemed to have given up on them and ran too. The reason? A huge crack was appearing along the cavern face.

With a great and thundering smash, the cavern face smashed apart, revealing a gargantuan and fiendish creature. Everyone turned to look at the awe-inspiring beast of chaos. Its skin was like lava, and glowed with gold heat of dark fire. Wings made of fire spanned from its back and on each wave of its wings flames burst forth. Upon its heads were two great protruding horns and its eyes glowed with an evil red as it glared upon the group of diminutive people below it. Then, it roared, its mouth sending almost unbearable heat around the cavern and then stomped angrily towards them.

What was of more annoyance to Leo was the small bolt that narrowly missed his foot. Below the creature were small, green and ugly beings. Each must have only been three foot tall, but they all carried black crossbows and were firing bolts in all directions.

"What is...?"

"Goblins," Alex interrupted Leo, "Not happy ones either. I'd have thought you would've asked about the giant infernal thing walking towards us."

"Too obvious," smirked Leo. The three of them ran back along the passageways, followed closely by both the stumbling beast and the many goblin-creatures. The three no longer cared about the Soul Light – just to get the hell out of there!

"Watch out!" Sarah suddenly called. Leo spun around and created an orb of glowing white light, and the bolts reflected off the energy surrounding the three of them. Alex meanwhile threw flame, incinerating the crossbow bolts before they reached them. Alex then stopped, looking at his skin as he felt the glowing fire inside of him. His heart was thumping fast and his eyes widened.

"What is it?" Sarah quickly asked.

"I... I made fire..."

"What – how?" Leo suddenly asked excitedly. Leo heard a scream to his left, and saw as Sarah fell to the floor, grasping her leg.

"Sarah!" Leo quickly shouted, looking at her bleeding leg and forgetting Alex completely. One of the crossbow bolts had hit her and it was deeply embedded.

"Oh no, I have to get this out," Leo said, about to reach for the bolt.

"We don't have time for this," Alex shouted through the rumbling of the caverns. "We have to get out now! Carry her!"

"Well, we have a distraction," Leo noticed, pointing down at the Black Mages who had foolishly tried to stop the huge beast and were being burnt and clawed, hacked to nothing. Leo picked Sarah up carefully, and the three continued to hurry.

Leo could have sworn he had no energy left, but his heart told him to keep going. If he wanted to live, and keep his friends alive, he had better keep moving...

XIII

A Scrap of Parchment

The distant screeches of goblins and the roars of the great beast were gradually moving closer and the rumbles ever louder. Eventually, the exit was near – the great doorway they had entered through at the very peak of the mountain's crater. Alex led them across the bridge that they had first crossed, when he suddenly stopped them. Leo knew why – he could feel his own skin begin to heat up like a wick to the flame. Leo looked down in terror and watched as great clouds of smoke and ash began to rise quickly, hiding whatever was underneath.

"This is no mountain, I can feel the fire now..." said Alex, turning to him and Sarah. "It's a volcano! Run! Go!" Sarah put each arm over Alex and Leo's shoulders and the three ran as strong and as hard as they could as the black smoke continued to rise up. They eventually reached the great doorway, covered in ash and with burn marks dotted around on their bodies and robes.

They all ran out with deepening breath, but the lava had reached the door's level. Alex jumped forward facing the door and braced himself. The wave of lava filled the doorway, but Alex was moving it through sheer power, stopping it from burning the three of them into a cinder. Leo watched in awe as Alex moved the wave back from the doorway, but Leo suddenly jumped back as lava started spewing from the edges of Alex's barrier. Alex was struggling to hold it off now – there was too much lava now.

"Sarah, c'mon, we're going up," Leo quickly shouted over the roaring and bubbling lava, "We'll meet you there Alex."

"Up? Why up? Are you insane?" shouted Sarah worryingly.

"It's too far down, if we go higher, the lava will burst over us and Alex and I can protect you. *Trust me*," Leo then added on seeing the distrusting face Sarah had. Sarah simply smiled, afterwards.

"I do, don't worry."

Leo, carrying Sarah, started to climb higher. Alex meanwhile continued to struggle with the lava as it pushed ever harder on him – even a Flamedra couldn't take this much strain. Alex gritted his teeth and placed all his effort onto the door, giving enough time for Leo and Sarah to get out of the way. Then, with them out of the way, Alex leapt upward and carried himself by a flame platform to Leo and Sarah. The lava burst forth like a caged lion and spewed down the volcano's side.

"Quickly!" yelled Alex, "Keep going upwards! Head for the crater!" Alex helped them both by conjuring a flame platform for them (which didn't even burn them) and raised them to the highest peak of the crater. Black smoke and ash continued to rise higher and higher. They reached the top and quickly made it to the edge, landing carefully.

"Ow!" Sarah then cried, as they landed.

"What's wrong?" asked Leo urgently. Sarah simply slowly put her hand down the side of her leg and placed it on the goblin's arrow. Leo removed the glove from his hand and placed a firm grip around it.

"Alex, keep the smoke away from us," he said. Alex nodded and stood above them ready in case the smoke approached them. Leo looked at Sarah, whose breathing was deepening with blood dripping quickly down her leg.

"I'm sorry, I have to take it out," said Leo, looking sorrowfully into her eyes at the thought of causing her pain. Sarah nodded, knowing it was best. Leo took a firmer grip on the arrow and then pulled it out, making Sarah scream for the moment.

"I'm sorry, Sarah," Leo quickly said afterwards.

"Why? It needed to be taken out," said Sarah, but her face still showed the mark of pain she had suffered. Leo nodded, but still felt guilty. The whole side of the mountain they stood on suddenly rumbled violently and in a rush a huge spew of lava burst upwards into the air and then started crashing down onto them. But, Alex and Leo both dived forward and created a small, but effective barrier, to cover them. The lava crashed down onto it, causing both Alex and Leo to cry out loudly – Leo now knew how hard it must have been for Alex. The lava was crashing down on the three of them and the strain began to grow on Leo. He could feel the magic in him draining fast and his arms burning with the energy being released. The lava then finally stopped spurting from the crater – wait, that wasn't supposed to happen.

Leo and Alex brought down the barrier to rest for the moment, but Alex rushed up to the edge of the crater. The lava had settled as a colossal smoking hot pool spanning across the crater.

"Something's not right," said Alex, looking down at the lava, "It should still be erupting."

"I can feel something," muttered Leo. He stood up weakly and moved over to Alex. "I can feel magic around it..."

The lava began to bubble in the centre and then something burst forth and upwards. It was the fiendish creature from the dungeon – it had survived the lava! The creature roared angrily, flapping its fire wings rapidly to stay in the air. Alex seemed to be mesmerised by the creature as he watched it roar ferociously towards them.

"I know what it is now," he muttered.

"You do?" asked Leo.

"Its name is the Chernobog," said Alex deeply, "They are creatures made from chaos and flame – once servants of my great god. It seems the Soul Light has a very suitable guardian."

"Well, we need to get rid of it, or else we're toast on its menu," said Leo. He drew his spear from his back but Alex placed his arm in front of him. Leo looked up at Alex – his eyes were glowing gold and red, like a literal fire in his eyes.

"This is my fight," he said, removing his torn shirt top.

"But – you need my help!" Leo shouted angrily.

"No, this is my test. I can create fire now – it is now that I test it. Please, I will not fail, Leo. I promise you that."

"Be careful then," said Leo, withdrawing his spear and patting Alex heartily on the back. "Kick its fiery arse."

Alex smiled, and his body was suddenly wreathed with flames surrounding his skin. He leapt up and the fire carried him towards the beast that raised its claw ready.

"I do not fear you!" Alex shouted angrily. The Chernobog's claw swept down, but Alex evaded it and then sent his fist at the beast. Leo first thought nothing would happen, but the very punch was of pure elemental power – the Chernobog was slammed upwards and it roared angrily again. Leo watched as it went to attack again with its claw, but instead Alex aimed his punch at its very claw – it recoiled as the pain struck its lava-like hand. Alex took his chance and spun round kicking the Chernobog strongly against the head and it fell down into the pool of lava. But it quickly flew upwards before becoming engulfed again in lava.

"Leo..." someone said. Leo quickly spun around to see Sarah, still clutching her leg. Leo slid down the rock side to her.

"What is it?" asked Leo quickly. Sarah was sweating, but not because of the heat. There was something else.

"Some – something's wrong..." she managed to mutter. Leo looked at the arrow that he had put down: there was green ooze-like liquid drooling down its tip. He then looked at the area around the piercing cut – the skin was turning a nasty shade of green and the veins around it seemed to have changed colour entirely.

"Oh no, it's poison..." he shouted angrily, "damn goblins!" He quickly and carefully took off Sarah's bag.

"Sarah, you're going to have to help me here," he added whilst taking it off, "what stops poison?"

"Erm... plantain..." she mumbled.

"Plantain?"

"It's... it's an herb mixture... it will be labelled..." said Sarah. Leo searched through the bag quickly and reached some small glass bottles. There was a mixture labelled as plantain, which Leo quickly uncorked. He put the mixture onto his hands and then gently rubbed it into the wound. Sarah winced painfully at the touch and closed her eyes tight.

"Sorry," apologised Leo.

"It's okay, I've told you this, just keep going," she replied. Leo continued regretfully and continued to rub the mixture in, his hands slowly becoming covered in her blood.

Leo glimpsed up at Alex, who continued to fight the Chernobog just as fiercely back. Alex was trying to evade the creature's attacks, but the Chernobog had caught Alex with its claws on more than one occasion. Alex now fought with the strength of fire, summoning the lava below into great attacking pillars that struck the Chernobog. Despite this, the beast continued its relentless attack regardless of the inflicted damage done. Many a time, Alex was almost overwhelmed by its attack. Nevertheless, Alex fought on with gritted teeth and flaming body – fighting the ultimate fight.

Leo kept glimpsing back and forth from Alex to Sarah, not knowing whether *either* of them would be okay. At times he wanted to leap out and fight alongside Alex, but he wouldn't be able to harm the beast – and the lava's boiling air would probably kill him. With Sarah, however, all he could do would be to wait as the herbs worked, which could take hours.

Alex and the Chernobog had split away from their last epic collision of attacks and both seemed to stare at each other for the moment. Alex was breathing deeply. Specks of hot lava dust were falling onto his skin but just melted on contact – sourcing him with power. The Chernobog roared angrily at Alex, but instead of turning to strike at him, flapped its wings towards Leo and Sarah. Huge dust clouds and boulders of rock were thrown from the crater's edge and Leo watched fearfully as it continued, pumping its wings ever harder. Leo dived to his spear with one hand and then quickly snatched up Sarah onto his shoulder with his other hand. He then slid down the mountainside quickly, away from the fight and far enough from the thrown boulders. Leo quickly peered up to see where Alex was, but all that remained was a huge fog of murky dust and ash.

CRASH – Leo ducked down as the sound rumbled along the mountainside, whilst Sarah let out an unexpected scream. Leo had to help Alex, definitely – something bad was happening up there.

"I'm sorry Sarah, I have to go," he said, kneeling down by Sarah, "Alex needs my help."

"That's okay," replied Sarah, brushing a finger along his cheek. She then stretched upward and pecked him on the check affectionately. "Be careful, for me."

Leo raced up the mountain with his spear carried ready, not knowing what he would see. As he reached the edge of the crater, he quickly cast a spell to rid his eyes of the smoke and to see. He reached the near edge of the crater.

Alex and the Chernobog had become locked in combat, their hands and claws grappling to overwhelm the other. Leo could only watch as they violently swung each other around, their muscles growing tired of the never-ending fight. At last, a winner was shown.

Alex released his grip and from his hands a columned fiery inferno was blasted down onto the Chernobog, it roared in pain and crashed down into the lava. It tried to swim upwards, but slowly it sank, the lava burning away at its wretched skin. It continued to rampage, struggling harder, and its claws swinging towards Alex but to no avail. Eventually, all that remained was its claw as it tried to grasp the air one last time – then, it was gone in the lava forever.

Leo looked at Alex in surprise, for he had come to look different from this fight. His body was wounded, his hair had become longer and spiked into the air. His body had changed, his muscles looked stronger and his skin seemed to glow an amazing gold – as if the very fire was in his pores.

At last, Alex turned to face Leo, a smile upon his face. The fire that lifted him into the air, allowing him to fly, was slowly fading away. He was still above the lava, yet the fire was diminishing – even the awesome glow of his body was failing him. Yet Alex continued to smile.

Then, the fire that once surrounded him vanished; Alex's body slumped, falling headfirst into the lava. Leo cried aloud and lurched forward, his hand pointed outward and holding Alex's body magically in the air. Alex's body was inches from the lava, and the hair Alex had was nearly touching the surface.

"No, I'm not giving up," said Leo feebly, his eyes watering as he watched Alex. The magic he had was failing him – Alex was slipping from his magic grasp. He could feel every drip of magic in him drain away, like going down a plug hole, as he issued forth to bring Alex towards.

Then, the magic left him and Alex fell into the lava.

"NO!" roared Leo, as Alex became submerged completely. "HE'S NOT GONE! ALEX! COME BACK!"

His voice was fighting with his mind – he couldn't be gone. He would appear, laughing: Alex was only making a prank. He wasn't gone – he wasn't dead like the Chernobog. He wasn't melting, his skin boiling away.

Leo wasn't sure how long he sat there, gazing miserably down into the lava, his eyes red and watering, hoping that Alex would reappear. But he didn't, and in his heart Leo knew he had to leave. If Alex was here, he would not have wanted Leo to wait around. His mind was regaining consciousness of the fact, and he remembered he had left Sarah waiting. Leo stood up, his heart aching painfully, and stumbled his way down the mountainside.

"Leo. . ." uttered Sarah, as he approached. Leo lifted her in his arms and carried her down the mountainside.

"Where's. . . where's Alex?" she asked and Leo was forced to stop. His arms were shaking and his eyes were stinging with tears that were nearly breaking through.

"He isn't. . . he can't be. . ." questioned Sarah softly, but she too realised the truth. Despite the pain in her, she raised a hand to her eyes and began crying silently. Leo tried not to cry, but his emotion was too strong and he felt tears drop from his eyes and trickle down his face, dripping onto the ground. Alex was gone. . .

– 0 –

It had taken a while to come down the mountain, but the cold mountain air had finally left. Night was falling, and Leo had set up a tent for Sarah due to her injury. Leo had spent most of the day sat silently, simply staring out into the distance. Somehow, he just couldn't take in that Alex was truly gone. He would even look back up the volcano, hoping to see Alex walking down after a second epic battle, but each time Leo instead found a greater sadness in his heart. He was dwelling in the past. He had to let go, to keep going and grow stronger. Leo sighed reluctantly at his choice and it took some time before Leo's mind was calm again and at peace.

Leo walked back to the tent, opening up to see Sarah, using more plantain on the wound. Leo sat down beside her.

"You okay?" he asked, looking at her leg wound.

"Yeah," she replied, rubbing the mixture in. "But, well, it's just hard to think that Alex is – is really gone." Sarah's eyes again filled with tears, but she quickly wiped them away; she was obviously suffering as much as Leo had been.

"At least he finally did what he wanted to do – he created fire, didn't he?" said Leo reassuringly, yet he found it hard to even reassure himself. Sarah nodded. She lay down under the blanket with Leo beside her.

"I'll miss him," she said miserably, staring blankly. "He may have been annoying sometimes, but he was a friend. That's all

154

that mattered." She smiled nervously at Leo, who smiled back and nodded.

"You and Alex have been my only true friends," said Leo truthfully. "I can't live without you two." Sarah giggled and blushed embarrassingly.

"What is it?" asked Leo, awkwardly.

"You've changed," she smiled, looking at him. Leo looked at her.

"Well, for the better!"

"Yeah right," laughed Sarah.

"Oh, is that so?" said Leo, grinning. He then grabbed her sides and started tickling her wildly, making her laugh and twist about.

"No! Stop!" she laughed loudly, Leo laughing at her as well. Soon, her cute laughter broke away slowly as they each looked into their eyes, their faces so close. Both their smiles had dropped as they gazed dreamily in stalemate. Leo moved his head forward, his hands still clutching her sides gently, and their noses touched gently. Then, he closed his eyes and their soft lips touched. After a long moment – or perhaps several hours – maybe years – they broke apart.

Neither of them said a thing as they lay there together, hand in hand, Sarah's head against Leo's chest. Just being there for each other, it was more than Leo could imagine, even contend with. Her warm touch against his body, like a miraculous dream.

It was a long time before Sarah finally fell asleep peacefully, yet Leo couldn't seem to sleep. There was a splinter in his mind, nudging him annoyingly – trying to solve some puzzle he couldn't see. Leo carefully slid away from Sarah's sleeping grasp and exited the tent, looking back happily at Sarah.

– 0 –

Something was not right. He stood, looking out into the distance as his mind raced with questions. This whole event: the jewel, the ambush, Alex's death...

Leo looked at the pearl in his palm, the so-called Soul Light. Leo gripped it in his palm tightly – his grip becoming tighter and tighter. After a few moments... it shattered.

155

He knew it. The jewel, it was just a decoy – a trap. For some, it would have been a surprise, but Leo had had enough surprises to last a lifetime already; this was nothing.

All this time wasted on an object of nothingness. All the travel, all the planning – weren't they on the right track? Draca told them it was here and seemed to know what it was. Was Draca fooled too? This Soul Light must exist – Eldred believes it to be, so does Draca, even the King's records. So why isn't it here? Why isn't he holding it now rather than a shattered decoy?

What could he do now? He couldn't return to Eldred without it. He would simply appear as a failure to him. Leo had already failed Eldred on many things – he didn't want to do the same again. He had to find it.

The worst thing, however, was the now present lurching of his stomach and the thought of Alex. If only he had realised sooner – meditated on the matter before entering the dungeon rather than been reckless – maybe he would have discovered the decoy. All of this could have been averted. And Alex... he could still be standing by Leo's side...

It had finally become apparent to Leo what could now happen to all he kept dear – he had already lost Alex, even Eldred had nearly been taken. Sarah had been kidnapped by Rais; it seemed so much was happening so quickly. And all because of one jewel.

Leo's decision had been made: he couldn't risk the lives of those he knew and loved for his own problems. He would take all the burdens alone – the Black Mages, the evil, the monsters, the beasts, everything. He couldn't bare the thought of losing another person in his life – he had already suffered that.

Leo walked back into the tent and from Sarah's bag took out her quill, inkpot and a scrap of parchment. As he wrote, he kept looking at Sarah tentatively, regretting what he was to do after what had happened tonight. He even felt a tear of sorrow tingle down his cheek. With every word he wrote, the strain became harder and harder. His hand began shaking as he wrote, not knowing if he would even finish.

Eventually, he completed it.

He returned the ink and quill into Sarah's bag, and took his own bag. He removed most of his food and water, leaving it lying inside the tent. He strapped his boots back on tightly, his gloves and his cloak. His spear was sheathed across his back, firmly in place. Leo looked at the ring on his finger, and wondered for a moment.

He took an arrow from Sarah's quiver and removed the ring from his finger. He carefully spent a few minutes scratching with the arrowhead's tip onto the ring, and then placed it in the folded parchment that he had written on. He took the parchment and carefully tucked it in Sarah's hand. She shuffled slightly, and for a moment Leo thought she might wake, but she remained sleeping peacefully. Leo couldn't help but stare at her, gazing at her beautiful face. Leo pecked Sarah on the cheek and walked to the tent door. He looked back at Sarah, regretting what he was about to do, unsure if he could do it.

He raised his hood, closing his eyes and left without a word into the midnight rain...

$$- 0 -$$

Sunlight shone brightly into the tent, a swift wind blowing gently across the ground. Sarah hoped to feel Leo's warm hands touching hers, but something stranger was in her hands. She leaned up from the covers, rubbing her sleepy eyes. Soon, the blurred image in her hands became a piece of parchment. She opened it in a hurry, wondering what it was. A silver ring dropped from the inside into her hand, and Sarah gazed at it. She recognised this ring...

She unravelled the parchment further until it was fully open and began to read:

Sarah,

The Soul Light was not in my hand last night. A shattered decoy now lies outside the tent, where I had broken it perhaps in my angered revelation.

I did not wish to do what I had to do, but I had no choice. I wanted to stay with you, be with you, kiss you again, but as long as the Soul Light remains out of my grasp you will be at risk. Alex's death showed this — if it weren't for me and the Soul Light he would still be alive. His death is my fault.

I have left what food and water I have to you. It should easily be enough for you and I know you will be fine travelling back to Arashar. I am sure Raiden will help you.

I wish things hadn't turned out this way – I wish none of this had happened. I will instead use the time that is given to me to find the Soul Light, but you will always be an ache in my heart. I truly regret leaving you, for I have become accustomed to you. In my heart, I came to realise the truth: I love you. And I know, whether by my will or fate, we shall meet again. I can't live without you.

Forgive me.

Leo.

Sarah stood transfixed at the letter; speechless and with tears filling her eyes. She couldn't think; she couldn't breath; her heart ached with pain. She felt the silver ring drop from her quivering hand to the ground near her tender feet. She knelt down and picked it up, wiping her eyes as she went. It was then she noticed something on it – something carved along its rim. She looked closer and read the sentence on it and, almost impossibly, a small but sobbing smile crossed her face. She twisted the ring onto her finger and read it slowly. It read:

I'll be coming back for this.